Praise for the Black Knight Chronicles

"Honestly, this is one of the best books that I've read this year and certainly a new series that I will be following from here on out."
—*Black Lagoon Reviews*

"I love this book. It makes me happy in a way that hasn't happened in a long, long time."
—Keryl Raist, Author of *Sylvianna*

Children are missing.

The police are stumped.

Halloween is coming, with an ancient evil on the horizon.

The vampires are the good guys.

This is not your ordinary fall weekend in Charlotte, North Carolina. Vampire private detectives Jimmy Black and Greg Knightwood have been hired to save a client from being cursed for all eternity, but end up in a bigger mess than they ever imagined.

Suddenly trapped in the middle of a serial kidnapping case, Jimmy and Greg uncover a plot to bring forth an ancient evil. Soon, they've enlisted the help of a police detective, a priest, a witch, a fallen angel and strip club proprietor to save the world. This unlikely band of heroes battles zombies, witches, neuroses and sunburn while cracking jokes and looking for the perfect bag of O-negative.

Hard Day's Knight

Black Knight Chronicles, Vol. 1

by

John G. Hartness

Bell Bridge Books

This is a work of fiction. Names, characters, places and incidents are either the products of the author's imagination or are used fictitiously. Any resemblance to actual persons (living or dead), events or locations is entirely coincidental.

Bell Bridge Books
PO BOX 300921
Memphis, TN 38130
Print ISBN: 978-1-61194-167-8

Bell Bridge Books is an Imprint of BelleBooks, Inc.

Copyright © 2012 by John G. Hartness

Printed and bound in the United States of America.

All rights reserved. No part of this book may be reproduced in any form or by any electronic or mechanical means, including information storage and retrieval systems, without permission in writing from the publisher, except by a reviewer, who may quote brief passages in a review.

A trade paperback edition of this book was published by Falstaff Books in in 2010.

We at BelleBooks enjoy hearing from readers.
Visit our websites – www.BelleBooks.com and www.BellBridgeBooks.com.

10 9 8 7 6 5 4 3 2 1

Cover design: Debra Dixon
Interior design: Hank Smith
Photo credits:
Christine Griffin

:Ldh:01:

Dedication

This book is dedicated to some of the fantastic teachers I've had in my life. Thanks for the helping hand and the kick in the butt.

Thanks to:

Marc Powers
Anne Fletcher
Blair Beasley
Ed Haynes
Deborah Hobbs
Kay McSpadden
William Good
Jan West
Durham Smith
Linwood Littlejohn
Billie Hicklin
Betty Dickson

Chapter 1

I hate waking up in an unfamiliar place. I've slept in pretty much the same bed for the past fifteen years, so when I wake up someplace new, it really throws me off. When I wake up tied to a metal folding chair in the center of an abandoned warehouse that reeks of stale cigarette smoke, diesel fuel and axle grease—well, that really starts my night on a sparkling note.

My mood deteriorated further when I heard a voice behind me say, "It's about time you woke up, bloodsucker."

Why do people have to be rude? It's a condition, like freckles. I'm a vampire. Deal with it. We can do without the slurs, thank you very much.

"Go easy on the bloodsucker, pal. I haven't had breakfast," was what I tried to say, but since my mouth was duct-taped shut, I sounded more like a retarded Muppet than a fearsome creature of the night.

My repartee needed work if I hoped to talk my way out of this. Of course, if my mysterious captor had wanted me dead, he'd had all day to make that happen. Instead, I woke up tied to a standard metal folding chair, the kind that gets sacrificed in countless professional wrestling matches. I tested my bonds. I was tied tight, and whatever he had bound me with burned—making him devout and the binding blessed, or the bonds were silver. My money was on silver. The true believers are more the stake-them-in-the-coffins types than the kidnap-them-and-tie-them-to-chairs types.

"Shut up, *bloodsucker*. You, as the one tied to the chair with silver chains, get to sit there and do whatever I say." My captor moved around in front where I could get a good look at him. I knew him, of course. It's never the new guy in town who ties you to a chair. It's always that creepy guy who you've seen lurking around the cemetery for a couple weeks in mid-October, the one that you can't decide if he's there to mourn or for some other reason. And, of course, it's always some other reason.

I'd seen this guy hanging around one of the big oak trees in my cemetery for a couple of weeks, near the freshest grave in the joint. I never paid much attention to his wardrobe until now, figuring it was close to Halloween, so he was just a goth kid getting a jump on the competition, but in retrospect I realized I should have. He wore almost stereotypical vampire-hunter garb. Black jeans, black boots, long black coat, wide-brimmed black hat. Christ, I bet he owned the *Van Helsing* Blu-ray. I swore then that if I ever got the chance, I was eating Hugh Jackman's liver. No, we don't usually eat people, but liver's a good source of blood, and I was pissed. I had been caught and trussed up like a Thanksgiving turkey by a skinny teen who watched too many bad vampire movies.

This kid was white, about sixteen, with mousy brown hair, and he looked like he played too much *Call of Duty* instead of getting a job. His skin was paler than mine, for crying out loud, and I'm dead. His clothes hung loose, like scarecrow garb, on his scrawny frame, and he either had an asthma inhaler in his front pocket or was happy to see me. God, I hoped it was an inhaler.

The kid reached forward and ripped the tape off, taking a layer or two of skin with it.

"OWWW!" I yelled, straining against my bonds. "You little rat bastard, I swear to God I am going to drink you dry and leave your body on the lawn like . . . like an empty bag of flesh!"

Okay, my similes need some work.

"I don't think so, bloodsucker. I think you're going to do anything I tell you to, or I'll leave you tied up there to starve."

He had a point there. It's not like there were very many people who would miss a vampire, and I hadn't yet figured out how to get loose from whatever silver-lined bonds he'd created. Sitting here and starving was entirely possible.

"All right, what do you want?" I asked. Might as well find out right now if he wanted something simple or—

"I want you to turn me," he replied. The look of hope on

his face was a little pathetic, really, but there was a determination there that was disturbing. Talking him out of his demand was not going to be easy.

"No." I wanted to get the short and simple part out of the way first, then we could move on to the lengthy explanations.

"Oh, but you will." He leered at me like a bad movie villain.

"Oh, but I won't." I just sat there. I couldn't do anything else, but one thing was certain—I was *not* turning this asshat into a vampire.

"I demand that you turn me. You are at my mercy and must do as I say," the asshat proclaimed. I craned my neck to see if there was an audience behind him. Nope, we were alone and he was performing for the rats in the warehouse.

"Not a chance."

"But . . . but . . . you *have* to."

"Not gonna happen, kid," I repeated.

"Why not?" He deflated like a Macy's parade balloon in a cactus field. Suddenly he wasn't a grandiose vampire hunter, but a scared teenager who'd caught a tiger by his toe and really didn't know what to do with him now.

"Because I don't turn people. Because this life isn't all it's cracked up to be. Because you'd miss all those romantical sunsets you probably write maudlin poetry about. Because it's not fair to the ecosystem to add another predator. Because we don't really sparkle. All of the above. None of the above. Pick a reason, kid, any reason you like. I'm not turning you." I started to look around for another way to get out of this mess, but it didn't look good for our hero. That'd be me since it's my story. Dammit.

For a skinny little gamer-geek, he'd done a good job tying me up. I guess that's another thing we can thank the Internet for—unlimited access to fetish porn has improved the knot-tying ability of men who can't get dates. I couldn't exactly see my hands, but by straining forward, I could see that my ankles were tied to separate legs of the chair with those plastic zip ties you get in the electrical aisle. I could see a silver necklace wound around each tie, and by the way my wrists felt, he'd done the same thing there.

The silver sapped the strength from my arms by contact, and I couldn't get enough leverage with my legs to do anything useful. I looked up to try and Jedi mind trick my kidnapper, when I noticed two things: one—he was wearing polarized sunglasses, which was a neat idea, although ultimately useless against my mental abilities, and two—he was crying.

"You have to turn me!" Tears streamed down his cheeks. "I'm running out of time, and this was the only thing I could think of to fix it!"

I couldn't believe myself. I was actually starting to feel sorry for the guy. "Okay, kid. Why don't you tell me what's wrong, and I'll see if I can help?"

"No one can help, but if I were one of the Undead I could help myself." I swear I could actually hear him capitalize *undead*.

"You know that's kinda my job, right? Helping people that can't help themselves. Kinda like the A-Team, without the Mohawk and the van. Reach into my shirt pocket and grab a business card. I promise not to bite you. The Undead cannot tell a lie." Total bullshit, but I've often found people dumb enough to romanticize the whole vampire thing will believe almost anything.

He reached into my pocket and took out a business card. It had my name, James Black, and cell-phone number under a logo—*Black Knight Investigations, Shedding Light On Your Darkest Problems*. Neither the company name nor the stupid slogan was my idea. And I prefer *Jimmy* to *James*.

"You're a detective?"

I nodded.

"And you think you can help me?"

"I can't really know that until you tell me what your problem is. So, why don't you untie me, and we can talk about this like a pair of reasonable people?" I put a little mojo into my eyes, and he started toward me with a pair of wire cutters in his hand. Then all hell broke loose instead of me.

Chapter 2

There was a huge crash from behind me, and I had a sinking feeling that my cavalry had arrived. I twisted around in my chair to see what was going on and watched as part of the roof came down in a shower of glass from the skylight and rotted wood. A rotund form struck the ground with a bone-jarring thump and lay sprawled on the concrete floor. From the curses emanating from the same general vicinity as the body, my suspicions were confirmed. My partner had arrived to save the day. With his usual subtlety and success rate.

"What the hell?" The kid stared at what had fallen through the roof, my freedom momentarily forgotten. I leaned forward onto my tiptoes and the front two chair legs and turned myself around to watch the floor show provided by my best friend and business partner, Gregory W. Knightwood IV. He's the "Knight" in Black Knight Investigations. Greg looked a little the worse for wear from his fall, but apparently none of the wood he fell on pierced his heart. Otherwise, I'd be looking for someone else to share naming rights with. After a few more seconds of muttered cursing, Greg realized that he had an audience and sprang to his feet, swirling his cape around him dramatically.

At least that was the idea. It's hard to swirl properly when part of the cape is draped over your head, but he gave it a hell of a try. Greg sometimes takes the whole vampire thing a little too much to heart. I was not surprised he'd chosen this moment as one of those times. In addition to the cape, he was dressed all in black spandex, which was not a good look for a guy who topped out at five foot nine and weighed somewhere around two-forty. He had on motorcycle boots, also black, and what looked like an honest-to-God utility belt. It was kinda like a cross between Batman and the Goodyear Blimp. At least Greg wasn't wearing a mask this time.

He fought with the cape for a few more seconds before finally mumbling something rude and tearing it to shreds. He looked at my captor with his most menacing stare and said, "Release my partner, and you might live to see another sunrise."

I thought that was a pretty good line under most circumstances, but Greg didn't know that the kid didn't want to live to see any more sunrises. Needless to say, he was a little taken aback when the kid lunged at him with a cross in hand. Greg stumbled backward a step before his vampire abilities outweighed his natural clumsiness, and he caught himself. Then he reached out, grabbed the cross from the kid and flung it across the room. The kid's eyes widened as he realized what kind of trouble he was in. Greg reached out and grabbed him by the throat, lifting him off the ground with one hand.

At least, he lifted him a couple of inches, because Greg was way shorter than the kid and didn't have the height to properly impress the wannabe vampire. Greg and the kid both seemed to realize this at about the same time, and Greg tossed him across the room in the general direction of his holy symbol. Then he came over to where I was bound and began to free me.

"Nice entrance." I smirked a little.

"You want to stay tied to the chair?"

Good point. I shut up and let him go about the delicate task of unwinding the silver from my wrists and snipping the wire ties. At least the kid had dropped the wire cutters close by so Greg didn't have to use his teeth. He'd freed my right arm when I caught a glimpse of movement out of the corner of my eye. I opened my mouth to warn my partner when he turned on the kid.

Vampires are fast. Like, ridiculously fast. And the first time a mortal gets a real eyeful of how fast we are, it usually freaks the person out. Not this kid, though. He was standing over Greg with a broken piece of lumber, probably what used to be a skylight, and Greg's faster-than-human whirl didn't give him a second's pause. He swung from the heels and cracked the board right over Greg's head with everything he had.

"Ouch," Greg said as he stared at my would-be kidnapper.

"You're still standing." The kid had a good grasp of the obvious, I had to give him that.

"Punk, the only thing you can do with that stick that will bother me is to shove it through my heart. And there's no way I'm just going to stand here and let you do that." Greg reached out and snatched the two-by-four out of the kid's hands. The kid tried to hold onto it, but Greg was way too strong for that. The board clattered end over end across the warehouse, and Greg passed me the clippers. "Why don't you finish the job? I think I need to keep an eye on your friend here to make sure he doesn't do anything else stupid."

I snipped the last plastic tie, shook myself free of the silver chain and stretched my arms and legs. Undead or not, being tied with your arms behind your back was damned uncomfortable. At least I didn't have to worry about him cutting off circulation to my extremities. I stepped to one side and pointed at the chair.

"Sit," I ordered.

"Are you going to turn me now?" the kid asked.

"No, but I am going to get a few answers, and I don't particularly care if you give them to me willingly or if I have to compel you to answer me." I'm not very good at compulsion, but he didn't know that.

"I'll talk, just don't hurt me."

I shook my head. The idiot wanted to be turned into a vampire, and he didn't think that was going to hurt? Kids these days. He sat in the only chair as I looked around for a stool or something and found nothing. Looked like Greg and I would be standing for the interrogation. Greg was poking through the kid's backpack, which was lying in the open trunk of an old sedan. Apparently that's how I'd been brought in, trussed up in the trunk of a Buick. Fantastic.

"Now, what's so awful that you want to be turned into a vampire to get away from it?" I asked.

Greg's head whipped around like it was on a swivel. "He wants *what*?"

"Yeah, apparently young Mister . . ." I paused and looked at the kid.

"Harris. Tommy Harris," he spluttered.

"Apparently young Mister Tommy Harris here wants to become one of the undead. He brought me here to turn him into a bloodsucking demon of the night. I haven't figured out yet if he has an unhealthy affection for the taste of human blood, or just doesn't like going to the beach, but that's why he kidnapped me."

"Wow," Greg said, slamming the trunk of the car and leaning on it. "He's dumber than he looks if he thought he could bully you into turning him. *Isn't he?*" Greg gave me an odd look, like he thought I might have actually turned the punk.

Greg is the only vampire I've created, way back when I was newly turned myself and not completely in control of my powers. Sometimes he picks inopportune times to play that guilt card.

"Yeah, pretty dumb." I decided not to air any dirty laundry in public and turned back to my kidnapper. "Tommy, what's going on that's so bad that you need to become a vampire to be able to deal with it? Maybe we can help. As I was explaining before my partner's unexpected entrance—" Greg sketched a rough salute from the trunk of the car, "—we are private investigators and we're pretty good at what we do. Maybe we can help you."

"I doubt it. I mean, I'm sure you guys are great detectives—"

"We are," Greg interrupted. I shot him a look that said *shut up, doofus* and gestured for Tommy to continue.

"But it's not a mystery you can solve by detecting, And I can't stop it," he finished.

"Can't stop what, exactly?" Greg reached into the top of his right boot and pulled out a blood pack. "Snack?"

"What flavor?" I asked

"O-positive. I didn't know what you'd be in the mood for, what with the whole kidnapping thing." He tossed me the bag, and I ripped it open. As I brought the bag to my mouth, I noticed Tommy looking even paler than before, which was no mean feat.

"What's wrong, kid? Haven't you ever seen one of us eat?" I turned the bag up and started to drink. Nice. This one was fresh, no more than a couple of weeks old, and while the bag smelled faintly of Greg's socks, being in his boot had kept the blood warm. It was smooth, obviously a young donor, without much in the way of contaminants, and the snack sped the healing of the burns the silver necklaces had made on my wrists and ankles.

"No, I haven't seen you . . . eat," Tommy said in a very small voice.

I finished the bag of blood and looked over at him. He looked like what he was, a very scared kid in over his head.

"Well this is a lot cleaner than the old-fashioned way, let me tell you," Greg finished off a blood bag of his own, and I wondered for a minute what flavor his had been. Each blood type had a unique taste, and different donors had their unique qualities, too. Finding a good batch in a blood bank was as likely as stumbling on a really good bottle of Bordeaux at Sam's Club.

Tommy looked a little sick, but he swallowed and went back to his story, careful not to look at either of us. "There's a witch that I pissed off, and now she wants to kill me and my whole family. All I could think of was to get you to turn me into a vampire so that I could kill her before she got to my family."

"Where did you find a witch in Charlotte, North Carolina? And what did you do to piss her off so bad she wants to kill you?" I asked. Our fair city is known for a lot of things—banking, bad basketball teams, good barbecue and car racing. But witchcraft doesn't even make the Department of Tourism's Top Ten list of attractions.

"And more importantly," Greg added, "how did you find out about Jimmy and figure out enough about us to nab him?" Greg hopped off the car trunk and was beside the kid's chair before he could even think about breathing. "Oh yeah, and we can smell it on you if you lie."

That's not exactly true. We can smell fear, and usually people smell a little different when they're lying, but this guy was so terrified already that I didn't think we could scent anything as subtle as a lie through all that fear. But he didn't have to know that.

"Well it all started with a girl," he began slowly.

Doesn't it always start with a girl?

Chapter 3

"She was just this weirdo little kid, all goth and stuff—"

Greg interrupted again. "Wait a minute. I thought goth went out in 1989?"

Tommy blinked before answering. "Uh... I wouldn't know. I wasn't born then. I know she wore a lot of black, too much eyeliner, always had on T-shirts with weird bands on them, you know, a freak." He didn't notice that Greg wasn't really listening, but was standing there shaking his head.

"I don't know, Jimmy-boy. I just don't know what's worse. The fact that you got captured by a human, or the fact that you got captured by a human *child*." Greg looked at me disapprovingly.

"Hey!" Tommy exclaimed. "I'm eighteen, you know. I'm no kid. After all, how old are you guys? You can't be more than a couple years older than me."

"None of your business—" I started, as Greg said "Thirty-five."

"Huh?" Tommy looked back and forth between the two of us, confused.

"Remember, kid? Vampires? Creatures of the night? We don't age, moron. We were turned when we were both twenty-two. Yeah, we're older than we look," Greg explained, reclaiming his perch on the trunk of the car.

"Except we're dead." I said, pulling over a stack of pallets and taking a seat. This kid looked like the long-winded type, and even with the blood, I wasn't feeling my best after being bound with silver. I decided I'd rather not stand for his whole monologue. "Anyway, you were saying?"

"Uh... yeah. Anyway, she was this weird middle-school kid or goth or whatever, and me and my buddies, well... we kinda gave her some crap from time to time. Nothing big, just—"

"Just making her life a living hell for the amusement of you and your idiot friends," Greg said, a grim look on his face. My partner had been heavy all his life, and middle school was particularly rough. An unfortunate side effect of becoming a vampire is your body never changes, no matter how much you eat or work out. Being trapped in an overweight body for eternity will give you sympathy for people who are picked on for being different. His stare never left Tommy's face as he waited for the admission of guilt.

"Um . . . yeah, I guess you could probably say that. But we were just messing with her—a couple of weeks ago—throwing her book bag around, popping her training bra and stuff, when this funky book falls out. It's all leather-bound, and soft, like a journal or something, and has writing on the cover like I've never seen before."

"I pick it up, and make to throw it to my buddy Jamie, and the girl goes nuts on me. She jumps on my back, pulling my hair and hitting me and stuff. She's never done anything like this, so I kinda shove her a little bit, not really even that hard, and she falls right on her butt in this big mud puddle, and the book maybe falls in the mud with her, and then she looks at me, and she curses at me."

He finally looked down, finally had the decency to look a little ashamed of his behavior, or maybe ashamed to have to own up to it to a couple of guys who were old enough to be his dad. But it wasn't enough shame to appease Greg.

"You mean, she called you a jerk, or an asshole, or something like that?" Greg asked. "Because, if you ask me, that was pretty well deserved."

"Nah, man, nothing like that," Tommy replied. "She really cursed me. She looked up at me and said something like 'By All the Dead, I Curse Thee. By All Hallow's Eve shall thee and all thy kin die a bloody death.' And when she said it, I could have sworn her eyes *glowed*, man. And I felt a chill run through me, and I knew she was for real. That's when I knew I had to get some serious firepower."

Tommy came to stand right in front of me and I could see the kid was way more scared of a witch in the future than two vampires in the present—and we could be pretty scary when we needed to. "Will you help me?"

"I don't know, kid."

Greg was less conflicted. "We don't usually go out of our way to defend bullies and kidnappers from justice. Seems to me you might deserve everything you're gonna get."

"I might, man, but my kid sister doesn't!" Tommy crossed to the Buick and grabbed Greg by the shoulders. "You've gotta help her, even if you don't help me. I mean, she's just a little kid. She doesn't deserve anything bad happening to her. If I get punished, that's fine. I screwed with the witch. I deserve to get turned into a frog or whatever. But Amy's only seven. She doesn't deserve to die because I was a jerk."

He was almost in hysterics, and I didn't want to see what would happen if he started crying and got snot all over Greg's costume. Lycra is a great fabric, but it doesn't shed mucus easily. I wish I didn't know that on so many levels. I also wished I didn't know where this was going.

As soon as Tommy mentioned a kid sister, he had Greg hooked. He's a sucker for cases with little kids. It goes back to his baby sister, Emily. That's a long story, and there's no happy ending, either. I was in as soon as he said "witch" because I'd never met a real one before, and I'm a sucker for cases with things I've never seen before.

Chapter 4

The next night a few hours after the sun set we were hanging out on Tommy's front porch waiting for him to finish dinner and lead us to the local witch's house. Or, more to the point, we were sitting on the roof of his porch so as not to scare his parents. I had to be careful to keep my feet from dangling off, and Greg had to be careful not to stray too far from structural support members. I wasn't sure what would have happened if he'd fallen through the roof, what with the rules about being invited in and all.

Falling into an abandoned warehouse was survivable. But an occupied personal dwelling? I didn't know if he would have fallen in and burst into flames, which would have been bad. We decided he should keep to the more solid parts of the roof.

It was about eight when the family fun time broke up, and our client made his way outside to meet us. He muttered some unintelligible collage of "out" and "nowhere" and "nobody" in response to his mother's queries, but eventually he stood on the sidewalk in front of his house looking around.

"Ummm . . . guys?" We let him stand there for a minute feeling nervous, and maybe a little silly, before we jumped down off the roof to flank him. At least I did. Greg, with his typical grace, managed to land half on the sidewalk, half in dog poop.

"Awww, man!" Greg gestured at his shoe. "Do you know how hard it is to get dog crap out of Doc Martens?"

"Bro, I didn't know they still *made* Doc Martens."

"Bite me."

"No thanks, pal. You went stale before the turn of the century."

He flipped me off, and I ignored him. "All right, Tommy, you're going to show us where this witch lives, and we're going to see if we can find anything out about her. If she's really a witch, we should be able to convince her to reverse the curse before anything bad happens to your family."

"How are you going to do that? You never said how you're going to convince her." Tommy was a nice kid, but a little whiny. I didn't need whiny clients. I had a partner for that.

"We can be pretty persuasive when we want to be."

"Remember? Creatures of the night? All that kind of nastiness?" Greg chimed in, having caught up with us after cleaning his boots. I'd talked him out of the spandex uniform for tonight, but he still had on the boots and utility belt. I'd decided to pick my battles on that front. And besides, every once in a while he pulled something useful out of his belt, like a flashlight, or tequila. My only concession to the stereotype was my long black leather coat, but I could get away with it the week before Halloween. Besides, I looked cool.

We walked along in silence for a while. At least, Greg and I tried to walk in silence. Tommy, on the other hand, decided to use this face time with the dark denizens of the night (his words, not mine) to satisfy his curiosity about the finer points of vampirism.

Block One: "Hey guys, is it true that you can't, you know, get it up unless you've fed recently? I mean, it makes sense, it is a blood flow thing." Cue sound effect of crickets chirping. The last thing I'm gonna discuss with a teenage wannabe is my erectile function. Or otherwise.

Block Two: "Hey, um, maybe this is too personal, but are you guys like, dating? I mean, I read somewhere that vampires are all, like bisexual and stuff. And you are always together." He finds it odd that the only two vampires in a city of a million and a half people hang out together a lot. You know, it is perfectly possible for two grown men to be roommates without there being anything out of the ordinary going on. Look at *Sesame Street*. No wait, that's probably not the best example. Just because you pay the bill does not mean you get the personal answers. And, um, *no*.

Block Three: "Um, do vampires poop?" Okay, maybe *this* is

the last thing I'm gonna choose to discuss with a teenage wannabe.

Thankfully, the witch only lived about four blocks from Tommy's house. One block farther and we might have had to rip out his throat to stop the interrogation. But he stopped and said, "We're here."

I stared at the typical suburban two-story house—nice wraparound porch, white vinyl siding, bike in the front yard, probably four bedrooms with one converted into an "office" where the dad surfed porn on the Internet while the mom watched *American Idol* in the den. It didn't look much like a haven for evil sorcery. We scouted the outside of the house for a while making sure there wasn't a doghouse or anything else that might screw the pooch on this operation.

Dogs don't like vampires. Cats usually just look at us funny, but they do that to humans, too. Dogs go absolutely nuts when they get near a vampire. They bark, howl, tend to pee all over the place, and depending on the size of the dog we're talking about, either attack or run like hell. Of course it's always the little yippy dogs that attack, and the big dogs with enough sense to run like hell. I've ripped apart my fair share of Chihuahuas in my day. After we made sure that the place was clear of pooches, we reconvened on the sidewalk in front of the house.

"Tommy, this is where you come in," Greg instructed. The kid looked stunned to be called on, like he didn't know whether to run home like he had a hellhound on his trail, or to charge in there and beat the little witch to death with a phonebook.

He took a minute to summon up his courage. "What do I have to do?"

"You've got to convince her to come outside with you to talk," Greg replied.

"Why?"

"Jesus, kid. Not everything you've read is true, but not all of it is wrong, either. We can't go in without being invited. And if she's got any kind of power at all, she'll sense that we're not exactly mailmen. There's no way in hell she'll invite us in. Now, go. Get to convincing." Greg put one hand on Tommy's shoulder and spun him toward the house. He put the other hand in the small of his back and propelled him toward the front door. I hopped up onto the roof of the porch to get a closer sniff of what this chick was and if she was anything out of the ordinary.

Tommy rang the doorbell, and a girl answered right away. I couldn't see her, but I heard her clear as a bell. "I knew you'd be coming. You may not enter, and your friends may not enter, either. Your pitiful life is over, Thomas Harris, and nothing you say to me will change that."

Her voice didn't sound right, like there was something bigger speaking behind her, and I could smell something that definitely wasn't teenage girl floating around. I felt a surge of power and hopped down off the roof just in time to see her try to slam the door in Tommy's face. That's when the kid did something I never figured he'd have the guts to do—he grabbed her. He reached inside and dragged her out onto the porch, slamming the door behind her.

Once she was outside, I figured this would be simple—we'd haul her back to our cemetery, scare the crap out of her, and she'd be begging *please-Mr.-Vampire-don't-eat-me-I'm-still-a-virgin* quicker than you can say garlic mashed potatoes. But as soon as I stepped up onto the porch I realized I was wrong. Again.

Chapter 5

I got to the porch a little before Greg, and we both stopped cold. The girl, who couldn't have been more than fourteen and a hundred pounds soaking wet, had Tommy on his knees. His left arm was hanging loosely down by his side, obviously broken. He wasn't screaming, but it wasn't for lack of trying. The silence had more to do with the fact that she had moved on from his arm and was busy crushing his throat with one hand.

I ran at her. She flicked out her other fist almost faster than I could see, and certainly faster than I could dodge. She caught me square in the solar plexus and doubled me up with one ridiculous punch. Lucky for Tommy she only had two hands, because Greg came at her the same time I did and landed enough of a punch to knock her a step backward, making her let go of Tommy's throat before she could finish strangling him.

"You should not interfere, vampire. There are forces at work beyond your understanding." Again, she used that creepy voice. This chick would have irritated me if I hadn't been scared shitless.

"Well," Greg said in his best placating tone, "we have interfered. Now let's talk about this like rational beings, shall we?"

Greg's always trying to talk his way out of fights. I think it goes back to being the fat kid in school. He couldn't fight, so he tried to talk or joke his way out of getting his ass kicked. I don't know that it's ever worked in all the decades I've known him. Didn't look like it was going to work now either.

The girl looked at him disdainfully, laughed and lunged at him with more of that crazy speed. She started throwing kicks and punches that made Jackie Chan look like a rank amateur, and it took everything Greg had to dodge enough of them to avoid being crushed.

I picked Tommy up over my shoulders and jumped him onto a neighboring roof. "Stay here, and stay quiet. I don't need to explain how you got here to the fire department. I'll come get you after we kick her ass." I made to jump into the scrap, but he grabbed my leg.

"What if you can't beat her?" he asked through a mouthful of blood. I missed the part where she busted his mouth up, but I guessed it could have happened when she switched from breaking his arm to choking him half to death.

"Then you don't have to worry about paying our bill." I jumped off the roof, cleared the front yard in one hop, and joined the rumble, which had moved out into the street. I didn't like the number of porch lights that were flickering on, so I stopped throwing punches long enough to say, "If you want to keep your presence here under the radar for more than the next five minutes, we might want to move this party somewhere more private."

"Or I could just kill you quickly," the girl said, nailing me with an uppercut that sent me flying into the path of an oncoming minivan.

"Or that," I said as the van crashed into my back (or I crashed into its front, whichever way you want to look at it). Greg took a kick to the head that spun him completely around, and she grabbed his head like she was going to twist it completely off his body. That's one of the only surefire ways to kill us, and when I saw what she had in mind, I reached deep down and did the only thing I could think of to save my partner's life.

I picked up that stupid little minivan, and slammed it into the freshman-from-hell with everything I had. Toys, glass, baby seats and a couple of yuppies spilled out onto the pavement, but the girl was finally down. Greg dragged the yuppies over to the sidewalk and dropped his Jedi mind trick on them about hitting a Great Dane and being cut out of the van by firefighters while I used their seatbelts to tie the girl's hands and feet.

There were more porch lights than ever flicking on now,

and I could hear sirens coming into the neighborhood. We had to move, and fast, or we were going to have some very uncomfortable questions to answer.

"Grab Tommy and get him to the hospital. I stashed him on a roof," I said to Greg.

"Where are you going with her?" he asked. He was weaving a little back and forth, but he could stand, at least.

"Where else? I gotta take her to Dad's." And I tossed the girl over my shoulder like a rolled-up carpet and took off toward the only place that was safe to interrogate her—St. Patrick's.

Chapter 6

I carried the girl/witch/thing over my shoulder toward St. Patrick's Church, hoping by all I had ever believed in that Dad could contain her. "Dad" is Michael Maloney, the priest at St. Patrick's, and he's one of the best friends a vampire could have. He's also an old friend, the only person from *before* that Greg and I ever associate with. He's been there for us for a long time, and I really hoped that he had enough juice with the Big Guy Upstairs to bind this whatever-she-was long enough to get some answers.

I couldn't go in through the front door. The holy ground thing is true. But there's a corner of the cemetery that sits on unsanctified soil, because the church decided during the Great Depression that it needed a place to bury suicides within the fence. That way the church could keep the funeral revenue. But, since Catholic doctrine wouldn't allow someone who took their own life to be buried on hallowed ground, they bought the property next door, knocked down the non-sanctified house that was there, fenced in the lot and expanded the graveyard. It's really handy to have a place to meet where no one would ever think to look for us, and Greg and I keep a room of sorts in one of the crypts for emergencies. And this was shaping up to be a doozy of an emergency.

I called Dad on my cell when I was close, and he met me at the crypt with a lantern and a battered leather bag. I guessed it was his exorcism tool kit and gave it a wide berth. Mike's never tried to douse us with holy water, but crosses, true believers and vampires don't mix. I steer clear.

"Jimmy, my son, what have you gotten yourself into?" Mike asked as he held the door for me. I dropped my little care package on the floor of the crypt and Mike stood there gaping at the hog-tied teenager in front of him.

"Don't call me your son, *Dad*. And I don't really know what I've gotten into. That's what I've got you for. This little chicklet is way more than she seems. She kicked the crap out of me and Greg both, and if I hadn't dropped a minivan on her head she probably would have killed Greg." That was the moment that my body decided to let all the bruises and exertion catch up with me, and I slid down to sit on the floor of the crypt.

"I don't suppose you've got anything to eat in that bag?" I eyed his satchel hopefully.

Mike shook his head. "Sorry, my—um—Jimmy. I don't exactly keep the red in with the Host."

"It's fine. I'll go out for a snack later. For now, we need to find out what's gotten into this kid. Literally."

Mike's eyes got wide, and he actually inched closer to his bag. "You think she may be possessed?"

"Not my field. But I know she's way stronger than she should be, and she sensed us as vamps from way farther away than even a bloodhound could have."

"Hmmm. Well, extra-dimensional beings would certainly be able to sense the presence of other creatures of their ilk, and demons are reputed to have incredible strength."

"Hey! Go easy on the demon talk, old buddy. Remember, me and my ilk used to slip you *Playboys* in middle school." I'd had issues with religion before I got turned, and since then I've spent most of my nights avoiding religious contemplation.

"No offense meant, James. It's just a term. Now, let me get a closer look at her." He knelt on the floor beside the girl, and only my speed allowed me to grab his shoulders and pull him back intact. The girl lunged at his face, trying for all the world to eat his nose. I yanked him out of the way, and the whatever-she-was laughed the kind of laugh that makes places inside you go very, very cold.

"Come closer, priest. Give us a little kiss," it mocked. Mike grabbed a crucifix from his bag, and thrust it at the girl-thing. It hissed and tried to roll away, but I lost sight of things for a minute. Probably because I was trying to put a sarcophagus between myself and the holy symbol. Mike was the truest type of true believer, and the cross in his hands gave me a monster of a migraine. From the looks of things, whatever was inside the girl liked it even less than I did.

"In the name of God the Father and Jesus Christ his Son on Earth I command you to leave this girl!" When I opened my eyes again, peeking carefully over the big stone coffin I was hiding behind, Mike was standing over the girl, cross in his left hand and a Bible in his right. The cross was glowing with an ethereal light, and it looked like something was floating around the girl. A cloud of what looked like glowing red gnats, buzzing and angry, coalesced around her head. Then I heard the voice again, and not for the first time that night, I got really worried.

"Foolish priest. Do you think that your trappings of faith can save you?" The disembodied voice was all around us, swirling in and out of the cloud like an angry wind. "I see inside your soul, priest. I see your darkest thoughts, your blackest fears, and you are *not* holy."

Mike raised his Bible over his head and pointed the cross at the girl like a conductor's baton. "I am a servant of the Lord God Almighty and by His Grace I am sanctified. You are a beast of Hell and I command you to leave this girl!"

The thing laughed, and I swear the girl's eyes glowed like a cheap *X-Files* effect. "I serve a power older and stronger than your pitiful little carpenter. Your little book means nothing to me, and you cannot command one with power such as mine."

Mike's Bible burst into flames, and he dropped the flaming holy book. He switched into Latin, and since I'm not old enough and certainly not religious enough to have much of a grasp on dead languages, I had no idea what he was saying. But after a couple of seconds of chanting, the cloud-thing screamed in rage and pain, and then flew at Mike like a comic-book bee colony, heading straight for his hand. The crucifix flared into blinding light, first white, then a deep crimson red. The voice sounded everywhere around us, and it began to laugh.

Through that awful cackling, I heard Mike howl in pain. There was one last flash of red light, and a wave of force blew out from Mike and the girl. Like a hurricane, it picked me up and flung me limp into the far wall of the crypt. The last thing I heard before I blacked out was that laugh. And Mike screaming.

Chapter 7

When I woke up, I was alone in the crypt. There was a puddle of melted silver on the floor where I last remembered Mike standing, and the seatbelts I had tied the girl with were lying in a pile in a corner. They'd been cut neatly, not torn, but that was all the info I could glean from my surroundings. I went to the door and eased it open a crack to see the bright sunlight streaming into the crypt from the cemetery.

Crap. I was stuck for a while.

The whole thing about sunlight is real, too. We don't burst into flames immediately, but it doesn't take long for one of us to be reduced to a pile of charcoal briquettes if we come into contact with direct sunlight. I settled down to wait for nightfall and hoped that Mike had recovered enough to go into the church. I decided to check on Greg and Tommy, and reached in my pocket for my cell phone. I pulled out a mangled mass of plastic and computer chips and realized that the phone had been crushed during my fight with the girl-monster. I hoped everyone was okay, because I was trapped until sunset.

After a ridiculously boring day of staring at a sunbeam, I felt more than saw the sun finally dip below the horizon, and I headed out into the cemetery. Mike was hurrying across the sanctified part of the graveyard to meet me.

"Where have you been, dude? I've been stuck in there worried sick all day!" I started to lay into him pretty solid, but then I got a good look at my old friend. He looked his age for probably the first time ever. He had a bandage on his forehead that looked fresh, and his left hand was wrapped heavily all the way from the elbow to the fingers. "Jesus Christ, man, how bad did she get you?"

"Pretty badly, I'm afraid. Not all of us are blessed with

eternal youth, James. I recently returned from the hospital with our young guest. She's terribly shaken up. I only got her to sleep in the parish house a few moments ago." He took my elbow and led me further from the church, as though there was someone in there he didn't want to take note of our little chat.

"What? She's in the church?" I was baffled. I would have bet the farm that she was way less welcome on holy ground than me. "And have you heard from Greg? My phone got—"

"Trashed. Again. Here." Greg tossed me a replacement phone as he came out from behind a tree. I looked him up and down, but he didn't seem to be any the worse for wear after getting pummeled last night. As if in answer to my unspoken question, Greg went on. "I'm fine. I had a snack before I went to bed last night. Tommy's arm is a clean break, but she got both the bones so it's gonna be useless for at least a month. They kept him at the hospital for observation. I talked to him while I was on my way over here."

I put the phone in my front pocket this time, since my back pocket didn't seem to be very good for protecting them. "What was that you said about the girl being in the church, Mike? I figured her for a serious bad guy, given what she did to all of us last night."

"What was residing in the girl was, in fact, a very serious bad guy, but the girl herself was guilty of nothing more than curiosity and a desire for a little payback on the kids at school who teased her. I think we can all relate to those sentiments, can't we?"

He raised an eyebrow at Greg and me, and we had the good grace to look sheepish. I'm not sure when my old friend had developed the juice to shame me for my youthful indiscretions, but he certainly had it now. Maybe it came with the first grey hairs. I'd never know.

"She was possessed? By what?" Greg asked.

"Yes, she was possessed. And based on the amount of power she exhibited, we may have a very serious problem. I don't know exactly what type of demon possessed her, but it's incredibly strong. I've never experienced anything like that kind of power. To be able to melt a symbol of the Lord in the hands of a priest . . ." Mike trailed off, and if anything, he looked a little paler. Not as pale as me, but getting there.

"How's the hand?" I didn't like seeing my old friend scared, and wanted to change the subject.

"Mostly second-degree burns. I dropped the crucifix before it completely liquefied, but some of the molten silver landed on my skin. I probably won't have full use of the last two fingers again for a while."

That explained the screaming I'd heard as I passed out. Molten metal eating through your flesh tends to make even vampires scream.

Getting one of my best friends injured and maybe permanently disfigured wasn't making me feel any better, so I switched back to the original problem. "So what do we know?"

"Not much," Mike said. "There are only a few demons that have the kind of power the girl exhibited last night, and all of them are bad news. And if what she said about serving an even more powerful demon is true, then we have to find where the demon went when it left the child, and stop it."

Of course we do. Because we're not vampires, the beasties that give people nightmares and make them think twice about walking down that alley alone, we're detective vampires. We're the good guys. Like Batman, only with dietary restrictions. Sometimes I wondered what it would be like to *eat* people, like a normal vampire. But no, not only do I have a conscience, I have a roommate with a Kal-El complex and a priest for a best friend. If I could find a shrink that kept office hours after sundown, I could spend eternity in therapy.

"What happened to the demon?" I asked.

"When you got it out of the girl it went back to Hell?" Greg asked, a little more hopefully than was reasonable.

Mike wobbled a little. "I have no idea, but I doubt it went anywhere we wanted it to go. I would expect that it found someone close by to inhabit, but the ethereal definitions of close by could mean anywhere in the city."

I led Mike over to sit on a headstone. It was a mark of how much had been taken out of him that he was willing to sit there.

Usually that was one of the things Greg and I did to get a rise out of him, sit on grave markers and make fun of the occupants. Mike never disrespected the dead. Greg and I exchanged a worried glance behind Mike's back, and I decided on an impromptu plan.

"All right," I said. "Mike, you stay here and keep an eye on the girl, and when she comes around see what information you can get out of her. Somebody had to help her bring this thing up. No kid has that kind of power. See if you can get the names of who else was in the circle with her that night, and keep her here. The beastie's gotten into her once. That might make her vulnerable to a repeat possession, if there is such a thing."

I motioned to Greg. "We'll split up and keep an eye on Tommy and his family. If getting revenge on him for picking on the girl was part of this creature's contract for getting to this side of Hell, then it may still go after them. I'll take the hospital, and Greg will keep an eye on the sister."

"That sounds good, boys. I think I would do well to do my part from my chair this time. Once I get there." Mike started back toward the church. "Boys?"

"Yeah, Dad?" I answered.

"Be careful. This one is bad. Very, very bad."

Greg and I looked at each other as Mike limped into the church, looking way older than we were supposed to be. We stood there watching our friend's back for a second, then headed off into the night for our respective charges. Good thing I was headed to the hospital. I needed breakfast *bad*.

Chapter 8

It only took me a few minutes to get to the hospital. By bus. I've heard that some of us can take animal forms, but either I haven't figured out how to turn into a bat, I haven't been around long enough, the vampire that made me wasn't strong enough, or something like that. I don't really know. Since I can't fly, I took the bus. And by that I mean I jumped on top of one and hitched a ride to the hospital.

I was out of cash. It wasn't that Greg and I were hurting for money. We did okay with the detecting business and it's not like we had much of a grocery bill, but I was bad about leaving the house without grabbing any cash out of the cookie jar, so I never had any money on me. That meant I rode the top of the bus a lot. It was more fun than mojo-ing the driver out of a free fare.

When I got to the hospital, Tommy had some company that I certainly wasn't interested in seeing—the police. I did a quick one-eighty in the hallway once I saw the guard outside his room and headed back downstairs to swipe a disguise. In general, it's a good idea to avoid masquerading as someone with medical training, because someone always wants you to do something with that training, and that can turn out poorly for you and the patient. So I usually put on my best janitor clothes and grab a bucket. There's never been a hospital that didn't have something that needed to be mopped, and the cleaning staff is usually invisible. Even if someone does notice you, they're just happy to see you working their floor.

I found an unattended supply closet on Tommy's floor and commandeered a bucket and mop. I wheeled my way down the hall to the room next to Tommy's, and headed in to mop and eavesdrop. Fortunately for me, the guy in the room was comatose and didn't care that I was doing a crappy cleaning job.

I was able to hear a grumpy-sounding female detective grilling Tommy through the wall.

"Mr. Matthews, how exactly did you break your arm?" she asked.

"Fell off my skateboard." Tommy had the sullen teenager thing down pat, probably because he wasn't acting. He *was* a teenager with a crap attitude toward authority figures and a system full of painkillers.

"That's bull!" I heard her slam something to the floor, and it didn't take a rocket scientist to figure out who was playing the bad cop. If she was playing. "The doctor told us your injuries were consistent with your arm being broken by a very strong person. Now who did it?"

"I told you, I fell off my skateboard." Tommy even managed a little whine at the end. I was impressed. I wasn't anywhere near that good at being a putz when I was a kid.

"And I told you, I know you're lying." I could almost see her leaning toward him. Her voice dropped and became confidential, inviting. "We can't protect you if you don't tell us the truth, Tommy. And you want us to protect you, don't you? I'd hate to have to leave here and take that guard with me. Wouldn't you?"

I certainly wouldn't hate that, but she wasn't asking me.

I heard nothing for a minute, then heard Tommy take a deep breath and say, "Okay, I'll tell you what happened." My heart, if it still beat, would have stopped for a second, and Tommy's next words did nothing to make me feel any better. Before I could reach through the wall and strangle him, he said "I hired a couple of vampire detectives to protect me from a demonic curse, and when we went to confront the witch that cursed me, she broke my arm like a twig."

The silence from the other room was thick, and I leaned my head against the wall berating myself for not eating the kid when I had the chance. After a long minute I heard the woman's voice again, and it was pretty obvious that she was not happy with Tommy's answer. She spit out the words like they were bullets. "You little bastard. I have somebody in this town kidnapping little kids, and this girl is the latest. Now, you were seen harassing her at school and the neighbors say a kid matching your description was at her house before she went missing last night."

"You know something about this. If anything happens to that little girl and it turns out you had anything to do with it, I will personally make sure that you do your undergraduate work at the federal penitentiary in Raleigh." With that, I heard her stomp toward the door. Seconds later I felt the wall shake as she slammed the door to Tommy's room.

"Come on, leave the chump here. Anything that's after him can have him," she said to the guard. Without a glance, they passed by the open door of the room I was mopping and headed for the elevator.

The woman led the parade, followed by two uniforms. She was striking more than pretty, a little too sharp in the face for most guys' comfort. Tall, with ass-kicking boots on she was almost six feet, her dark brown curls tied into a messy ponytail. She wore a tailored jacket open to show her badge and gun, and a cross around her neck.

I notice the little things, like crosses. They get to be important. I counted to a hundred twice and then wheeled my bucket into Tommy's room. He was fiddling with the bed when I closed the door behind me and moved a chair under the knob. I didn't need any nurses coming in to take fluids while Tommy and I had a heart-to-heart.

"Holy crap!" Tommy cried. "I almost peed the bed! I thought you guys had left me here to die!"

I crossed the room as quickly as I could, which is pretty damned quick, and put my hand over his mouth. "You want to yell that a little louder? I'm not sure every brat in the nursery heard you," I whispered into his face. His eyes got big as he noticed the pointy teeth, and I backed off a little. "How long were they here? What did they tell you? Start at the beginning and walk me through."

"They were here when I woke up. That chick cop was a real bitch. She was all about wanting to know how my arm got broke, but I didn't tell her anything, I swear." He flopped back onto his pillows looking proud of himself.

"Except the absolute truth, you mean. Good thing for all of us she's a civilian and doesn't believe in anything having to do with our world." Tommy looked a lot less smug, and I cocked an eyebrow at him. "Vamp senses are ridiculously good. I listened through the wall."

I pulled a chair over to the window and looked down. The detective was standing by her car looking up at me. I sat down quickly hoping that she was nearsighted. I knew I'd have to deal with her before this mess was over. She wouldn't see a vampire and think "janitor." Not this one.

"Did she say anything earlier about little kids being kidnapped?"

"Dude, don't you, like, read the paper?" Tommy used the remote to elevate his bed so he could see me better after I took the chair.

"My morning delivery leaves a little to be desired. Enlighten me."

"There's been, like, ten or eleven kids go missing in the last month, dude. There's talk of not letting anybody go out for Halloween unless they catch whoever's taking them."

That would suck. Halloween is one of the best nights of the year. It's like a Vegas buffet, only everyone you nibble on has had so much candy they all taste like dessert. I took the lid off his dinner plate and poked around at the leftovers, hoping for a little Jell-O. "Go on."

"What are you doing? I thought you couldn't eat."

"Old habits. Now about the kids?"

"Oh, yeah. Well, the first couple were no big deal, their parents were all over each other about custody anyway, so most folks figured one or the other was lying and had swiped the kid. But then a pair of twins vanished out of a day care, and people started to get worried. By that time, everybody was making a huge deal about the cops not caring because the first kids were black, and the latest kids were white, and it got to be a whole big thing. The cops made a task force and held press conferences, and made a big news thing out of everything. But while the cops were conferencing, kids kept disappearing. Hey, can you hand me that ginger ale?" He took a drink while I looked at him.

"Is that all?" I asked when he didn't continue.

"What do you mean? I guess. That's what I know, anyway."

Sometimes I wonder if everybody in the world is brutally stupid, or if it's just my clients. "Your demon and this bunch of disappearing kids might be connected."

"No, man. That was, like, a demon or something. This is just some kids going missing. Oh! I get it! You think the demon might be taking the kids, right?"

It's almost cute how excited stupid people get when they figure something out. Like Christmas for morons. "I was thinking that maybe the people calling the demon might have something to do with the vanishing children, yes. How many did you say were gone?"

"I don't know, man. They were all little kids, like middle school. I didn't really pay attention, 'cause I didn't know any of them. But I did kinda know this girl whose little sister got kidnapped. I think they said she was number eight or something like that."

"Does your friend have a name?" I had the beginnings of a plan, but I needed to be able to leave Tommy alone and know he was safe. He was a moron, but he was my moron for the moment.

"Dude, she's not my friend, I barely know her." I motioned for him to go on, because I didn't care. "Janice Reynolds. My buddy Rick used to go out with her or something. Or maybe hooked up with her at a party. I can't remember. But she lives in that new development over by the high school. What are you gonna do?"

He held out his ginger ale and waited. I finally put it back on the tray for him. I hate pretend invalids.

"I'm going to go talk to your friend Janice. But I've got a couple of other stops to make first, and I need to make a little noise so your guard will come back. Try to make this convincing."

"Make what convincing?"

I didn't answer. Instead I put a pillow over his head and counted to twenty. He thrashed around pretty well, but wasn't anywhere near smart enough to press the call button for the nurse. After he passed out, I made sure that he was still breathing, pressed the call button myself and threw the armchair out the window. I figured that would be enough to draw attention even at a hospital, so I wheeled my mop bucket in the opposite direction from where all the people were running and ducked into a stairwell to make good my escape.

Chapter 9

I walked past the crowd of people looking at the armchair that had crushed the hood of a police car in front of the hospital and headed toward the bus stop. The cop car was a nice touch, if I do say so myself. I thought my luck was finally starting to look up as I got to the bus stop, but my phone rang and proved me wrong again.

"Yeah," I said.

"Dude, you gotta get over here!' Greg sounded more than a little freaked out, but he freaks out when he burns a Pop-Tart.

"Slow down. One, where are you? And two, what's up?"

"I'm at Tommy's house, and the cops are here! They're talking to his parents about a string of kidnappings. They think Tommy might be involved, and they're talking about taking him out of the hospital and arresting him!"

Great. "Is there a woman detective there? Tall, ponytail, boots, attitude?"

"Yeah. She's a real ball-buster, man. She's got Tommy's mom in tears and his dad all freaked out about college scholarships and lawyers and that crap."

"Don't sweat it. She'll be leaving any second."

"What are you talking about? Wait, there she goes. How did you . . . ?" Greg trailed off.

"I'll explain later." I looked up and down the street, really wanting a bus to arrive before Detective Kickass got back to the hospital. "Now here's the plan—go knock on the door, and when Tommy's dad answers, mojo him into not seeing you, then deck him. Leave him out cold in the doorway, and then break a couple of windows. Get the hell out of there and meet me at home. We've got work to do."

"What?!?" I held the phone away from my head as Greg

freaked out again. I counted to ten, and when he paused for breath, I put the phone back to my head.

"Do it, and meet me at home. I'll see you in half an hour." I hung up, and when I didn't see a bus anywhere, stepped out into the street in front of an oncoming car. The poor banker-type slammed on the brakes, and I pulled him out of the car. He started to say something, but then took a look in my eyes and fell silent, like a rabbit staring at a wolf.

I didn't plan to snack on him, but it had been a long night, and I was still really hungry. And that deer-in-the-headlights look got to me. I grabbed him by the tie and pulled him in. I spoke to him, not really saying words, just noises meant to calm the prey while I sniffed the side of his neck, smelling the fear-sweat and listening to the blood pulse in his carotid.

I took a quick glance around at all the cars in the parking lot, all the people milling around, and decided this would really have to wait. I looked into his eyes and whispered, "Sleep." He sagged like a sack of slightly overweight potatoes, and I tossed him into the passenger seat of his BMW SUV. I hopped in the driver's seat and headed off toward home with a plan in mind and dinner next to me.

I didn't go all the way home, obviously. There are good ideas, and there are bad ideas. And for vampires, leaving a car with your last meal in the front seat parked outside your lair definitely falls into the "bad idea" column. I drove to an alley behind a biker bar called The Thirsty Beaver a couple miles west of our place and got into the back seat behind my meal. He was still out cold, so I grabbed his left hand and brought the wrist to my mouth with little fanfare.

Feeding is a basic need, and not deserving of androgynous and mildly homoerotic adjectives. A man's gotta eat, plain and simple. And what this man has to eat is human blood. I normally would have raided the blood supply at the hospital, but all the police there had made that a little too high profile for my tastes.

I pulled his wrist to my mouth and licked the place at the bottom of his forearm where the veins run closest to the skin. I used the left wrist because between the rapid healing inherent to vampire bites and the fact that this yuppie wore an expensive watch, I figured there were better than even odds that he would never notice he'd been snacked upon. Not that anyone would believe him, but I tried to keep things neat when I could.

My canines extended into razor-sharp points, and I tore as small a hole as I could while still letting the blood flow. It splashed against the back of my throat all hot and coppery, and the thick syrupy liquid went down as smooth as twenty-year-old scotch. And as a matter of fact, I could taste a little hint of scotch. Somebody had been driving while intoxicated—bad boy.

It had been a while since I drank from the source, and it was *good*. Greg doesn't approve, so whenever we're together I drink from the bag, but man, there's nothing like the taste of fresh blood right from the vein. It's hot, with that metallic and salty taste that's like nothing else in the world. We can live on blood bank supplies, but it's the difference between a really good rare filet mignon and a frozen hamburger patty. I drank for a couple of minutes, just a couple of pints, and then leaned back in my seat behind the yuppie, who was still out like a light.

"Was it good for you?" I asked my sleeping dinner. He was as silent as I expected him to be, which was good for both of us. I probably would have flipped out had he woken up at that exact moment, and it's usually not a good idea to be the human trapped in a car with a freaked-out vamp. I took a minute to make sure I hadn't dripped anything on my shirt, steal the snack's wallet and leave him behind the bar. The Beaver had enough hipster traffic that one more SUV wouldn't draw too much attention until closing time, and by then I'd be miles away.

I tossed his wallet minus the cash in a dumpster and headed home. Now I had bus fare to get home on, but since I was close, I took it at a quick jog and was there in fifteen minutes without breaking a sweat. The four-minute mile is a big deal to human runners, but it's pretty much a warm-up pace for dead guys.

Greg was waiting for me when I got home, and he was practically bouncing off the walls. "Apartment" is a generous term for our home, I suppose. We live in the basement of a caretaker's house in a local municipal cemetery. Municipal cemeteries work best for our brand of lurking, because they're not consecrated ground. We can hang out there. Greg and I figure we can cycle through as the "caretaker" every dozen years or so, just to keep the folks that own the cemetery from getting suspicious about the fact that we don't age. We fixed up the basement with a couple of hidden entrances, and outfitted it the way we wanted. The caretaker's cottage is decorated in vintage redneck, so anyone stopping by sees exactly what they expect to see. On they go, and no one gets in our way.

I made up some story for the cemetery owners about being an insomniac writer with an online poker addiction, so they leave me alone when I never go outside in the daytime and am up all night. They don't really care, as long as the graves stay mowed and clean, and I subcontract that work. As long as we don't charge anything for our "maintenance services," they don't charge us anything to live there. It's a pretty sweet deal, if I do say so myself.

"Dude, what the hell took you so long? I've been going nuts here waiting for you!" Greg had an Xbox controller in one hand, but hadn't even bothered to turn on the game. He usually crushes the games, but obviously tonight he was more interested in what I had to tell him.

"Sorry, had to stop for take-out on the way." I sat beside him on the couch and picked up the second controller. "What are we playing?"

Greg was having none of that and grabbed the controller out of my hands. "No frickin' way, man. What is the deal, and what are we going to do about that man-eating woman cop?"

"I don't know what the deal is yet, but I'm starting to get the idea that our little demon chasing Tommy is just the tip of the iceberg. And I'm pretty sure that our distractions will keep the detective out of our hair for a little while. Hopefully she'll be busy chasing after whoever busted up Tommy's house and jumped out the window of his hospital room long enough for us to get to the bottom of all this."

"But I busted up his house, and I guess you broke his hospital window . . ." My partner's book smart, not street smart, but he's damn loyal and has super-powers, so I keep him around. Besides, he's been my best friend since sixth grade. We met getting stuffed into adjacent lockers in gym class. Even then, his was a tight fit.

"You broke the hospital window," Greg repeated as understanding dawned on him.

"Now you get it. So we need to find out everything we can about these kids that have gone missing. Tommy said there were ten or eleven of them, and that's why the cops were after him so quickly. You get online and see what you can dig up, and I'm going to go interview the sister of one of the earlier kidnap victims. Then we crash for a little while and try to catch up with Dad early tomorrow night. Sound good?"

"Works for me. Hey, did you bring any leftovers with you from the hospital? I'm getting a little peckish." Greg headed over to his desk and its brand new MacBook, external monitor setup and a ridiculously large array of external hard drives. Greg's on a mission to collect every vampire movie ever made, so he needs serious storage. He uses more bandwidth in a week than most of Nebraska uses in a year, so it's a damn good thing he figured out how to piggyback onto the network of the bank headquarters down the block.

"Sorry, dude. No leftovers. Not even a drop to spare." And it was true. My donor would probably have felt really crappy when he woke up if I had drunk any more. I wasn't lying to Greg exactly, just avoiding a repeat of the fight we always have when I drink straight from a human.

He barely even looked up from his keyboard as he muttered "Pig" at me. By the time I'd gotten to my closet he had four Firefox windows open with a different Google search running on each one. I swear I think instead of super vamp-speed he got super-fast typing when we got turned.

I went over to my closet and started weapon loading for bear. I usually only carry one good knife, a Marine-issue Ka-Bar tucked into the back of my belt, but this gig had been anything but usual to this point. I put on my shoulder holster and grabbed my Glock 17. I checked that it was loaded with silver bullets, and put a spare magazine of silver ammo in my back pocket. The silver load was for anything supernatural we encountered. I knew how much the touch of silver hurt me, so I figured nothing else in the magical world would like it, either. It meant I had to wear gloves when I loaded my magazines, but I considered that a small price to pay. I loaded the holster with two spare magazines of regular ammunition, and strapped my backup to my right ankle. I carry a Ruger LCP for a backup when I think things could go really bad, and everything I'd seen in this case told me things could go from "peachy" to "holy crap" in the blink of an eye. I put another knife on the other ankle, rolled my jeans down to cover all the hardware, and straightened up, reaching for my black hoodie. Greg had turned away from the computer and was sitting still, staring at me.

"How bad do you think this is going to get?" He suddenly looked as worried as I'd seen him in a long time, and I sat on an arm of the couch and looked at him.

"Bad. I don't know what we're up against, but if what was in that little girl isn't the boss, and I don't think it is, then whatever is running this operation is even meaner."

Greg sat back in the chair and sipped on a juice box. I don't know where he picked up that habit, because all it did was make him pee purple half an hour later, but he was hooked on the silly things. After a long sip, he said, "Then guns and knives aren't going to be a whole lot of help, are they?"

"Probably none at all," I admitted. "But on the off chance that they might be useful, I think I'll bring them along. Besides, the really bad guys use human pawns a lot of the time, and guns and knives work fine against humans. That reminds me." I reached into the floor of the closet and grabbed a couple of spare magazines for my LCP backup pistol. They went into a jacket pocket.

"Man, you can't go killing humans just because they front the bad guys. We have to be sure. What if they got suckered into working for a Big Bad?"

"I know. I know. If I take out any humans, I promise to verify their complete and utter evilness first." I might have grinned a little, but just a little.

"I just meant—"

"I know what you meant. I promise not to kill anyone that doesn't deserve it." I held up one hand, three middle fingers together. "Scout's honor."

"You were never a scout. They wouldn't let you in."

"Objection, your honor! Relevance!" That got a chuckle out of him. "I promise I won't kill anyone who's not a bad guy. We cool?" I started toward the stairs.

"Yeah, yeah. Hey Jimmy?" I stopped, not turning to look at him. I knew what he was about to suggest, because I'd already thought of it. He was right, of course, but I didn't want to think about it.

"Do you think we should talk to Phil?"

"Probably." I still hadn't looked at him. I could feel him looking at the back of my head, and it was a little itchy.

"Then you're going to talk to him now?"

"Only because I have to." I hate dealing with angels. They always make me feel so damn *unclean*.

Chapter 10

I've never been a fan of strip clubs, and I'm even less of a fan of angels, so putting the two together is so far out of my comfort zone it's like dropping Huck Finn into Times Square. I walked across the parking lot into Phil's place, shaking my head, as always, at the blue neon sign flashing "Heaven on Earth" to the passing traffic. I paid the cover, flashed my library card at the bouncer and mojo'd him into thinking it was a driver's license. I'm not terribly photogenic, and I haven't renewed my license since the early nineties. Putting the whammy on people is easier. I took a seat at the bar and tried to order a beer, but a pair of six-inch Lucite platform heels kept getting in the way. I finally waved the girl down to me, slid a dollar in her garter, and she jiggled on down the bar to more interested parties.

A different night, a different case and maybe I wouldn't have waved her off, but this wasn't the time or the place. Especially not the place. Fiction vamps that sparkle and fixate on true love give the rest of us a bad name. I don't sparkle, I'm no more perpetually horny than anyone (or anything) else, and I don't use my vampire powers to get laid. I'm not even particularly angst-ridden, and don't know any vamps that are.

I ordered a Miller Lite and told the bartender I needed to see the boss. He waved a thirty-something woman over who bore all the signs of an ex-dancer who had moved up, or at least sideways, in the world. "I'm Lil, I'm the manager here. What can I do for you?" She slid onto a stool next to me. Dark hair cascaded down her back and she was dressed in black leather from head to toe. Her eyes hinted at some undefined ethnicity I couldn't place.

"I didn't ask for the manager, Miss. I asked for the Boss." I put a little emphasis on the last word, hoping she might pick up on the idea that I knew more than the average lap-dance customer.

"As far as you need to know, kid, I *am* the Boss." She raised me an auditory italics and returned my verbal capitalization with one of her own. When she looked me straight in the eyes, I got a little hint that there was more to her than a fading stripper with aspirations of earning a GED.

"Is there somewhere we can talk?" I asked, looking around at the gyrating bodies. It was loud, but not so loud that I wanted to risk someone overhearing me go into the supernatural aspects of life.

"Follow me." She slid off the stool and walked towards a dark alcove with VIP in pink neon over the doorway. I now understood how the neon industry was staying alive. Apparently it's all being used in strip clubs. I followed her and noticed that the view of Lil from behind was, in a word, incredible. Ex-dancer or not, she still had plenty to show, and the tight black miniskirt she was wearing displayed it very well. Naturally, I thought the most covered woman in the place was hotter than any of the naked ones. I've always been a sucker for a little mystery.

We walked down a black-carpeted hallway with doors on only one side. Each door had a light over it. Some were red, some green, and one was blinking yellow. Before I could ask what the caution light was for, Lil said over her shoulder, "Time's almost up in that one."

I didn't want to think too much about what was going on inside the rooms, and I didn't have to, because past the room with the blinking yellow light Lil opened a door with no light over it. I hadn't even seen the door from the hallway, but when we entered, I realized it led into a spacious office complete with desk, a sofa, a full bar and a bank of monitors that covered the club, the parking lot and all the VIP rooms. She motioned me toward the chair facing the desk as she went over to the bar.

I didn't sit, preferring to lean against the desk and watch her make the drinks. Not only was the view better watching her than the monitors, but it kept her in my line of sight. In my business there are a few ways to get really dead really fast, and turning your back on people you don't know in their lair is near the top of the list.

"Can I get you anything?" she asked as she poured bourbon over ice for herself.

"No thank you."

"Are you sure? We have beer, wine, B-positive, holy water."

I went for my Glock the moment she tossed "holy water" into the list, but instinct kicked in too late. She'd already picked up a small pistol hidden on the bar and pointed it calmly at my heart.

"Don't get frisky, little vampire. It's loaded with silver rounds, and you don't want to know what that will do to you. Now sit down. I'm not going to hurt you. If I wanted to do that, you'd be dead." I didn't take my eyes off the gun until she walked around the desk, sat down, and put it in a drawer. Her left hand was out of sight somewhere under the desk's surface, and I had a sneaking suspicion that the pistol was the least of my worries.

"Okay," I said, sitting, "you know what I am. Is that a problem?"

"Not for me. But you wanted to see the Boss, and he's not a huge fan of vampires. That could be a problem for you." She sipped her bourbon, and it took all I could do not to lean over to look under the desk.

"I'm not a huge fan of angels, but Phil and I have done business before." I shifted in the chair so that, in an emergency, my crossed leg could block most of my center mass from anything but a shotgun blast. I really hoped she didn't have a shotgun. It probably wouldn't kill me, but it would be damned inconvenient. And messy. "He knows me."

"Indeed, I do, James," said a polished voice from behind me. "But I still need to know why you're here."

I jumped almost high enough to touch the ceiling, and when I came down I was standing facing Phil. His manager and her firearm fetish momentarily forgotten, I leaned heavily on the edge of the desk.

"Sweet baby Jesus, Phil. If my heart still beat, I'd have had a heart attack. The whole teleporting thing is one thing, but sneaking up on people is not cool, man."

Phil was dapper, as always, in a black suit tailored to his lean frame. Phil and I were similarly sized, well over six feet tall with broad shoulders and thin builds, but he always looked better than me. It helped that he was a lot more muscular than me, and could afford a tailor.

Girls think angels are dreamy for a reason. He was ridiculously good-looking even to a straight vampire. My hair is kind of mousy brown and sticks out everywhere, but Phil's dark wavy curls always fell perfectly into place. He looked like a print ad for men's hair product, only three-dimensional and annoyingly real.

Phil was right in my face before I stopped babbling. "You know I don't like that name used in my presence." Behind the rage in his eyes I saw something deeper, some kind of regret maybe, something that moved him on a visceral level.

In a rare moment of sanity, I decided not to push. I broke off eye contact and looked down. "Sorry about the J-word."

"Apology accepted." Phil backed off a little and I could breathe again. "Now I owe you an apology of my own for startling you. Please let me offer you a drink. One without a threat. Lilith, would you please provide our guest with a drink?"

He and Lilith shared a look, and I could almost feel the power struggle between them. Just as I was starting to feel uncomfortable, the name hit me.

"Holy crap!" I bounced back to my feet. They both turned to look at me, and I stammered, "Y-you-you're Lilith? *That* Lilith? Like Eve before Eve, but you-wanted-to-be-on-top-and-you-got-banished Lilith?"

She looked at me very coldly, then walked around the desk and stood right in front of me, almost as close as Phil had a moment before. She looked me up and down and said, "That is one version of the story. There are others."

The way she said "others" let me know the story I knew wasn't remotely her version, and that her version probably didn't appear in any of the books I'd ever read, or would ever read. Honestly, I didn't think I was too interested in hearing her version. The look in her eyes promised that if she told me she'd have to kill me.

Breaking the silence, she smoothly asked, "Now, would you like a drink?" She brushed her hair back off her neck and tilted her head to one side in preparation for me to bite her.

Holy crap and sweet baby Jesus.

"Ummm . . . thanks, but no thanks. I've already had dinner tonight." I tried to step back, but my ass was already pressed up against the desk. I had nowhere to go.

"Please, I insist. It is a rare honor my Lord has offered you. If you refuse you dishonor his gift and pass up an opportunity seldom given to one of your kind." She spoke so low it was almost a whisper.

Looking into her eyes I thought for a moment that this must be how a mundane feels when I mojo them. It was almost like my will wasn't my own, except that I knew the choice was mine. The people I whammy don't weigh the consequences of their choices. I did.

I put my lips to her neck and breathed in the scent of her hair, and knew that I would drink. Her hair smelled like everything I missed about being alive, sunsets on the beach, summer afternoons in a park, fresh-cut grass, that intoxicating scent of salt, beer and cocoa butter combined that defines a weekend at the beach. I buried my face in the side of her neck and held my mouth there for a moment, feeling the pulse under my lips.

"You don't have to be gentle," she murmured into my ear. Then a hot spike of pain and pleasure ran down my neck as she bit my earlobe.

Gentle left the building. I sank my teeth into her with no concern for her well-being, because I knew that whatever she was, I certainly couldn't kill her. She put one hand behind my head and held my mouth to her neck, while the other hand wrapped around my waist to rest on the small of my back. Feeding for me has never been a particularly sexy thing. I've never been much for mixing sex and dinner, but Lil was different. The taste of her exploded into my mouth, and I saw colors as my eyes rolled back in my head.

I've drunk from stoners, winos, psychos, schizophrenics and club kids hopped up on everything from acid to ecstasy to the best coke to ever come out of Bolivia. Every substance you can shoot, snort, smoke and swallow makes its way into the blood. But nothing I'd tasted did justice to Lilith's blood. I'm not sure there is a substance that could, and, if there is, I don't think I want to know what it is. Addictions are dangerous.

I took the smallest sip from Lilith, and I thought the top of my head was going to blow off. Every hair on my body stood on end, and spasms went through every muscle.

I stood there with my mouth latched onto her neck twitching like a kid that just peed on an electric fence. The light show going on behind my eyelids was a Pink Floyd wet dream. I drank from her for only a couple of seconds, but I stood there draped over her, gasping and letting her hold me up for several minutes while I came back to earth. It's a good thing Phil didn't have any grudges against me, because if he'd wanted to stake me then and there I couldn't have done anything to stop it. Which is why addictions are dangerous. They lead you to stupid behaviors. I try not to be stupid too often.

After a long moment I got my breath back enough to gasp out, "You're an asshole, Phil."

"You didn't like it?"

I could hear his smirk in the tone of his voice as clearly I could hear the undertone of harp music. "Yeah, I liked it. It was incredible. The best thing I've ever had. And I never want to taste anything even close to that again."

I straightened up and walked on rubbery legs to the bar and poured myself two fingers of a very expensive scotch. The last thing I wanted to do was put anything in my mouth that would erase the taste of Lilith's blood, but I knew that if I didn't start forgetting that taste as fast as I possibly could, I'd keep putting off drinking anything. It wouldn't take long for me to starve out of fear of losing that amazing taste. I slugged back the scotch and poured myself another.

When I felt like I could look him in the eyes, I turned to face Phil. "What's the deal? We've done business before without any of the games. What's different now? Why the snack?"

Phil took a seat behind his desk and gestured toward the chair I'd vacated when he popped in. I sat, and he slid a coaster across to me. I should have known I wouldn't be allowed to do anything so coarse as to put a glass on his desk. He waited for me to arrange my drink, then said, "Things have changed, James. The balance of power in our fair city is in flux, and it is not in my best interest to align myself too closely with either side."

"I don't get it." I figured there was no point in trying to play mind games with an angel, fallen or not. Regardless of our respective brain sizes, I was giving up a few thousand years experience to Zepheril (or Phil when I was being obnoxious, which was always). I went with honest ignorance, which has served me well so far.

"There is a new player in town, James. A player with the potential to shift things significantly to one side or the other. And until I see which way the wind is blowing, I have decided that it would be unwise to make any specific alliances."

"Who? Lilith's new in town, but she's working for you. Who is it?" There was obviously something going on between them, but she looked way too much like she was the slave to his master, at least this week.

I decided I had read that situation right when he leaned back in his chair and laughed. "Oh no, James. Lilith is my servant, at least for the moment. She is here as a result of a wager. A wager that she lost." Lilith didn't look very happy about that. Phil waved her over and gestured imperiously, and Lil sat on his lap like a very sexy and very dangerous kid with Santa at the mall. Only this Santa was a fallen angel, and this kid was older than Eve herself and had more issues than *Reader's Digest*. "I speak of a tectonic shift in the balance of power, a change that may not only herald change for the city of Charlotte, but for the world as a whole."

That didn't sound like anything I was going to like. Still, I had to ask. "Does this power have anything to do with my having to fight a possessed little girl last night and the missing kids all over town?"

"As usual, you have managed to find yourself in the middle of it all. In parlance you might understand—you've brought a knife to a gun fight."

I hate being right.

Chapter 11

I took a minute to digest what Phil had said, and then decided this was going to warrant another drink. I poured my third scotch and returned to my seat. "What kind of power are we talking about, Phil?"

"I don't really know, James. I only know that since the children have begun to disappear I have sensed a power growing in our fair city, and I have watched it with no small interest."

Phil reads too much. I mean, seriously, who talks like that? It irritated me, and that didn't bode well for the rest of my evening. "So you don't know anything that could help me find it, fight it or kill it. Or if you do, you're not going to tell me because you think it's stronger than me, and if I go after it all I'll do is piss it off, and you're afraid if I poke the big scary bear that you'll be facing off with something that you don't want to take on."

"That is a fair summation of the facts, yes." Phil's voice went a little cold, and there was a warning in his eyes that told me not to push this.

I don't like being told what to do. It makes me itchy, and when I get itchy, my mouth runs away from my brain. I knew better than to poke Phil too much, so I turned to Lilith. "What about you, Little Miss Sunshine? Do you know anything about the Big Bad? Or do you think we should sit on our asses and eat popcorn while Rome burns, too?"

Lilith looked at me through half-lidded eyes from her perch on Phil's lap, and I actually blushed. I didn't even know I could blush anymore. I'd assumed vampires didn't have the blood flow to spare. I assumed wrong.

"Little vampire, tread lightly. There are forces at work here that you cannot even imagine. I suggest you go back to your little hole and play your video games. You do not want to be involved in this."

"No, I don't. I definitely don't want to be involved. I'm no hero. I'm just a guy trying to make a living, buy a few video games, and maybe find a nice fresh neck to gnaw on now and then. But like it or not, I am involved. There's a scared kid out there who I promised to help, and as stupid as it sounds, I try to keep my promises." I looked at both of them with as much humility as I could. "Please, tell me what you know, and I'll get out of here and back to trying to save the world without getting my ass kicked too bad."

Lilith chuckled, an earthy laugh that made parts of me tingle that didn't tingle very often since I had become a bloodsucking fiend. I was starting to get a pretty good idea where her powers lay, and I gotta admit, they were impressive.

She got up off Phil's lap and came to sit on mine. She twined herself around me in a remarkable imitation of a wetsuit, and it took everything I had to keep focused. "Little vampire, if you insist on your own self-destruction, you will never be able to taste me again. Is that really what you want?"

"No," I said in a small voice as I watched the gleam in her eyes grow into an inferno. "But it's what I've got to do. Sorry, honey."

Her gaze turned cold, and I could imagine her ripping my heart out with her bare hands and feeding it to me. My newly tingly nether regions stopped tingling.

The moment my body's Fun-O-Meter hit fear instead of interest, she stood up, flounced back over to the corner of Phil's desk, and sat down in a huff. "So be it," she said in a voice like a frosty January window.

Phil leaned forward slowly as if struggling with a decision. Finally, he said, "We are not entirely sure what is coming, but there is a major summoning in process. It requires the exchange of thirteen pure souls for the souls of thirteen of the damned."

"Children would qualify," I said unhappily.

"Whoever is performing this ritual must have some plan for the thirteen damned souls, and it seems to involve Samhain somehow."

"Of course." I chimed in. "It has to be Halloween, which is in a matter of days. Because it's not bad enough that there's a gigantic evil thing about to rise from the Hellmouth and devour us all, there has to be a time limit so we can wrap all this up and go to commercial. I hate Halloween."

Phil just stared at me for a moment.

"Sorry," I said. "But some days it really feels like I'm trapped in an episode of *Buffy the Vampire Slayer*."

"Your legs aren't that good," Phil said. "May I continue?"

I nodded.

"There have been eleven kidnapping victims to date, and their bodies have been inhabited by the souls of the damned. Until you interfered and released the latest damned soul into the city."

He had me there. I had been the one to ask Father Mike to dispossess the soul with extreme prejudice. "Yeah, that wasn't exactly my best moment. Do you know what happens to that girl now? Last I heard she was a little freaked out, but in decent shape."

Phil steepled his fingers and leaned back. "She will be susceptible to possession unless your friend the priest is able to provide her with some type of shielding. The soul you cast out of her will not be able to return. But she will be more likely to see and hear the presence of souls around her than a normal child."

"And if she continues to dabble in the mystic arts?"

"She will undoubtedly end up dead long before she finishes puberty."

I hate how much that bastard knows about everything. Or maybe it's that I hate having to drag it out of him. He's a bazillion years old, tied to all the bad guys in town and has ridiculously high-speed Internet. The least he could do is not make me beg for scraps. It's a game with him. I'd better know the right questions, or he won't play.

"And the soul?" I asked.

"The soul will look for a host. Typically it will inhabit an empty body, but if one is not available, it will attempt to possess one weaker than itself."

Lilith looked like she might jump into the conversation, but a glance from Phil shut her up. Then we were back to playing Phil's little game. It was time to see if I'd asked enough of the right questions, and if I could be trusted with the answer to the big question. "And how do I stop who—or whatever is behind this whole mess?"

"I don't know. To know that, one would have to uncover exactly who is performing the ritual and what they expect to gain. With that knowledge, then you might be able to stop them."

Phil stood, and gestured toward a door that I was pretty sure hadn't existed until that very moment. "But you will, as I said, have to accomplish that without my help. For I have given you all the aid I am interested in giving you, and now you must go."

One day I'll figure out what powers the fallen have and how much of their power is mojo like mine, but this obviously wasn't going to be that day. I'd pushed as much as I dared. Gotten as much as I could.

Lilith opened the door, and stood very close as I made my exit. "Farewell, little vampire. I do hope you enjoyed my . . . hospitality."

I blushed again as I went through the door and found myself in an alley behind the club. I felt a little dirty, like I'd been caught drinking the Communion wine or something. I hadn't, for once, but my Catholic upbringing always left me a little self-conscious about anything that felt that good.

Chapter 12

I took a moment to regroup, which wasn't easy. I was outside a high-class strip club with a tummy full of immortal hottie blood and a killer buzz. My to-do list now included figuring out what the hell an XYZ ritual was, did, or caused, and of course now I knew that I was on a tight deadline. Halloween was looming just a few days away, and I couldn't exactly go to the cops for help.

Interviewing the family of the victims seemed easier, and probably safer. I decided to do that first. Tommy had given me the address for Janice Reynolds, the older sister of Victim Number Eight, before I left the hospital. I didn't mind the drive. It was all the way south of town in the ritzy Ballantyne area. Ballantyne was a new development built around a golf course nobody could afford to play on and a resort hotel nobody could afford to stay in.

The houses were typical Charlotte pre-recession McMansions with postage-stamp yards and more room in the garage than Greg and I had in our whole basement apartment. The whole neighborhood was pretty boring, except for the token over-decorated holiday house on the corner, with ghosts in the trees and an eight-foot-tall inflatable pumpkin in the front yard. When I found my particular McMansion, I took a quick lap around the house to make sure there was no private security. There were no cops still hanging out, so I knocked on the front door, pointedly ignoring the cardboard Dracula hanging over the peephole.

A fiftyish man answered, and by the way he stood halfway behind the door, I was pretty sure he had a gun in the hand I couldn't see. I didn't blame him. His youngest kid was missing, presumed dead, and the bad guy hadn't been caught. I guess if I was still alive and in his shoes, I'd be a little jumpy, too.

"Mr. Reynolds?" I asked.

"Yes. Can I help you?" He didn't open the door any wider.

I stayed a few feet back from the door on the porch, trying to look as innocent as possible while keeping a little in the shadows just in case this guy was perceptive enough to see through my youthful appearance to the experience behind it. I hoped this would be one of the times that being turned at an early age was an asset. I got mistaken for a high-school kid more often than I enjoyed. Tonight I'd play the high-school kid for all it was worth.

"I'm Tommy Harris. I go to school with Janice, and I wanted to stop by and see how she was doing, what with everything that's happened to you guys and all." I must have nailed my impression of a living high-school senior, because he stepped back and held the door open for me.

"Come on in, son. I'll get Janice."

I stepped across the threshold and felt the familiar tingle that I get whenever I go into someone's home. I've never understood the invitation requirement, but it's as true as sunlight and stakes. We can't enter a private residence unless we're invited, which means Greg and I don't make many house calls. We try to meet our clients in public places so we don't run into any uncomfortable situations. But since Mr. Reynolds had issued the invite, even under false pretense, I was in.

"That's okay, sir. Can I go up?" I could hear the girl open a door upstairs and didn't need her coming down to blow my cover. Dad had tucked his gun away somewhere, but I wasn't certain I could get it away from him before he did enough damage to ruin my night.

"Sure. How did you—"

I left him there asking questions as I took the stairs two at a time. I saw a slim blonde girl at the top of the stairs wearing a pink T-shirt and sweatpants. She took one look at me and got a very confused look on her face.

"You're not—"

I put my hand over her mouth and moved her backward toward her room. I had crossed the last few feet between us with super-human speed, because, well, I'm not human. She hadn't expected that, which actually shut her up a fraction of a second before my hand landed.

"Don't say a word. I'm here to get your sister back," I whispered in her ear as I steered us into her bedroom.

The décor screamed twenty-first-century teen girl chic, with a poster of Lady Gaga over her computer desk and a picture of Edward Cullen over her bed. I have to give Team Edward credit. Despite his sparkling, the Twilight kid has done wonders for vampire public image.

"Can you keep quiet? Because I'd like to let you go, but if you scream, I'm going to have to jump out your window, and I ruin a lot of jackets that way."

She nodded, and I took my hand off her mouth. Of course, she instantly opened her mouth to scream. I grabbed her by the arm and pulled her down to the bed. All the air went out of her in a *whoosh*, and she sat there gasping, eyes wide. I sat in the computer chair and quickly shut down the machine. The last thing I needed was some webcam running or IM client popping up in the middle of our conversation.

"Now will you be quiet? I could have hurt you there, but I didn't. And I won't. My name is Jimmy, and I'm a private investigator. Here's my card. I'm working on the kidnappings, and I'm trying to get as much information as I can to help bring everyone home safely. I'm not a cop, and I don't work for your dad, so nothing you say will get you in any trouble. I just want to help you get your sister back."

"What's in it for you?"

I didn't expect that. "What do you mean?"

"I mean that ever since Lauren went missing we've had private eyes camped out on our front porch, promising to find my sister for money. We've had psychics, drug dealers, snitches, bounty hunters and every other kind of asshole you can think of beating down our door. And now I'm supposed to believe that you want to help because it's the right thing? Bullshit."

This was a cynical kid. I guess I understood where she was coming from, though. I took a deep breath, put on my best

I-shouldn't-be-telling-you-this face and gave her my best answer. "I'm not doing this for free. Don't worry, I'm getting paid. By whom is none of your business. Maybe one of the other families is loaded and they want their daughter back. I need to know everything about every abduction to get their kid back, and if I rescue a few extras and get my picture in the paper, all the better. So I get paid, you get your sister back, and everybody's happy. But I can't help your sister if you draw attention to us. Deal?"

She croaked out "Deal," and we bumped fists. I might be old, but I have a television, so I know Howie Mandel's shtick as well as anyone.

"Now, what do you know about who took your sister?"

"N-nothing. She went to school like normal, and never came home."

"She made it to school that day, stayed the whole day, left on time, and never made it home, that's the deal?"

"Yeah, from what we can find out. The cops aren't telling my parents much, and they won't tell me anything. I've had to eavesdrop and snoop around to find out anything at all. It sounds like she left school like every other day, and somewhere between school and here, just vanished. I don't know who would want to steal Lauren. She's just a little kid. She's kind of obnoxious sometimes, but she's a sweet kid, and I don't know why anybody would want to hurt her."

She started to sniffle, and I sat down next to her on the bed. I'm not exactly good with crying girls, so I put one arm around her shoulders and kinda hugged her like that for a minute until she seemed to get herself together.

Sitting there with her reminded me of going to Greg's house for Thanksgiving and hanging out with his baby sister. She was younger than Janice, but she always loved her big brother, and was pretty wild about her "Uncle Jimmy," too. I sat there holding the crying girl and thinking about what I'd lost all those years ago, and it became very important to get her sister back.

"Are you okay?" I asked after a minute. I really hoped she

didn't get any snot on my jacket. It was my favorite one.

"I think so."

"I don't think they took your sister for anything she specifically did. I think she was taken for what she is. All the kidnapped children have been around the same age, between nine and thirteen."

"What does that matter?"

"Some religions have something they call the age of innocence, where children are still free from sin. Some folks believe that young kids are inherently innocent, and innocence is valued in some rituals. I don't understand it all, but it's a theory we're working with."

"Do you think my little sister was kidnapped by *Satanists*?!?" Her voice went up a little, and I put my hand over her mouth for a second. I really, really didn't want her dad coming in just then.

She was freaking out, and I was worried that any more noise and he'd do exactly that. Time for Plan B. I had all the information I was going to get from her, anyway.

"Sleep." I made my voice very heavy and looked deep into her eyes as I said it. She shook her head once, as if to shake the cobwebs loose. Then her eyelids fluttered once, twice, and closed. I laid her down on the bed before she could fall off, and made my exit. I closed her door quietly and got almost to the front door before her father's voice stopped me cold.

"Tommy?" he called from the den.

Crap. I held my ground in the entrance hall. "Yes sir?"

"Are you leaving?"

"Yes, sir. I could tell Janice is still really upset about Lauren. I decided to head on home."

"Yeah, there's a lot of that going around. Come in here."

Double crap. I could smell the whiskey from my spot by the front door. He was hammered and his oldest daughter was sleeping off a dose of vamp mojo. His youngest child was missing, and God only knew where his wife was. I owed him the simple courtesy of listening, if nothing else. I might be dead, but I remember how to be a decent human being.

Mr. Reynolds was sitting in a well-worn tan easy chair with a bottle of Wild Turkey on the end table beside him. The Kickin' Chicken was a serious step down from Phil's Glenlivet, but I was pretty sure I was going to find a way to accept a highball glass of rotgut sometime in the next three minutes if it were offered. "Are you all right, Mr. Reynolds?"

"Call me Bob. And no, I'm not. Sit down." He waved towards the couch.

I studied him as I took a seat. I only needed a second for the once over. He screamed past-his-prime-bank-vice-president, which sounded like half the over-forty population of Charlotte. Thinning hair, going grey at the temples even though he was barely into his fifties Casual clothes for a night at home, a polo shirt and crisp khakis rather than old jeans and a faded T-shirt.

He was pudgy, but looked like he exercised a bit, maybe tennis and golf to try and keep the bulge away. He'd missed a spot while shaving that morning, and that little chink in his armor, coupled with the Wild Turkey, told me he was falling apart fast.

And, why not? He'd had his soul ripped out and stomped on right in front of him.

"Can I do anything to help, sir? Should I maybe call Mrs. Reynolds?" I couldn't stop the question even though the last thing a smart vampire would do is waste time playing nursemaid and/or father confessor.

"You could bring back my baby girl, that would help." His dry laugh was a lot closer to a sob than any sound of mirth. "And as for Mrs. Reynolds, well, I don't know if she'll be any easier to find than Lauren. She said she was going to her mother's, but I haven't heard from her in two days."

"I'm sure she's just trying to get her head on straight, sir."

"Yeah, I'm sure that's what it is."

"Look, Mr. . . . um . . . Bob, I've got to get going. I've got school tomorrow and—"

He cut me off with a wave of his hand. "Don't bother. I know Tommy Harris, and I know you're not him. I suppose you're a reporter or something?"

"No sir, I'm a private investigator. I've been retained

by . . ." I trailed off, trying to come up with one of the other victim's names, but it had been a long night. I came up blank.

" . . . one of the other families. I'd hoped that your daughter could remember some additional facts to help my investigation."

"Son, don't bullshit a bullshitter. I'm in sales, and I can smell BS a mile away, and let me tell you, what you're spreading will make the roses grow but it won't help bring my little girl back. Now, I want to tell you one thing. Whatever you want to write about me, go ahead. I'm not the world's best dad, no matter what my coffee mug says, but you write one word about my little girl and I will absolutely destroy you." He leaned forward for emphasis and almost fell out of his chair.

Usually I don't react well to being threatened by anything lower than me on the food chain, but I couldn't help but feel a little sorry for him. I said "Yes, sir. I will keep that in mind," and headed out the front door. I felt an unfamiliar sense of responsibility. These people's pain was real to me now, and I had to do something. So I started walking to where it all began.

Chapter 13

It only took me a few minutes to walk to Lauren's school. Going to the last place she was seen made sense. I could try to pick up any bad vibes, or smells, or even maybe a clue. Ballantyne Elementary School was a sprawling brick building with a cute little portico in front, where parents dropped their kids off when it rained.

I poked around the campus for about half an hour, hoping a heretofore unknown special magic-detecting sense would kick in or that there'd be a huge pentagram drawn on the roof of the building. Instead I found a whole pile of nothing and was about ready to trek back to the main road to hail a cab or unsuspecting solo driver when inspiration struck.

I whipped out the new phone Greg had given me and dialed him up. He answered after the second ring. "Hey, what are you doing, bro?"

"Trying to hack into the police department database to get the case files. Why, what do you need?"

"Two things. I need your super-sniffer, and I need a ride."

"Where are you?"

"Ballantyne Elementary, down south."

"What are you doing, looking for a date?"

"Classy. Just come get me. I'll explain on the way home."

I hung up the phone and sat on the roof of the portico to wait. About twenty minutes passed before headlights turned into the drive. I stood up on the roof and started to wave when I realized that the headlights didn't belong to Greg's car, or to mine. I dropped flat to the roof as a police cruiser pulled into the drive and parked in front of the school.

Great. I'd apparently picked the one school in the district with enough money for motion sensors on the roof. I lay as still as I could while the cop got out of the cruiser and did a lap around the building, shining his flashlight into the windows. I grabbed my phone and shot Greg a quick "stay away, cops are here" text before switching the phone to silent and returning it to my pocket.

After the second lap the cop got back in his car and just sat there. He left the dome light off, but I could see him fingering a picture in his sun visor. He sat there for a long few minutes before driving off. I texted Greg an all clear, and he pulled up in front of the school a couple minutes later.

I waved him up to the roof, and he vaulted to my side in one easy leap. I'll give him credit, the boy is not the exact image of grace and fashion, but for a chunky nerd vampire, he's handy to have around.

"Give this place a sniff," I said. We all get super-senses, but at different levels. Greg's sniffer is better than mine, I hear better than he does. He's stronger than me, I'm faster than him. And as far as we know, neither of us can turn into bats.

Greg sniffed the air for a minute. "There's something funky in the air, but I don't recognize it. Now tell me again why I had to drive all the way out here to get your sorry butt."

"Because there aren't any buses to Ballantyne at two in the morning, I don't really have the dough for a cab, and I didn't want to steal any more cars this week." I jumped off the roof and walked over to Greg's car. He followed me down and unlocked the car with the remote. Greg loved his classic hot rod, but he loved modern conveniences and gadgets more, so his GTO had keyless entry, remote start, a badass stereo and seat warmers, which are more useful than you'd think for the cold-blooded.

He slid into the driver's seat and started the car. "Fair enough. Hey! What do you mean steal any *more* cars? I thought we agreed that we were the good guys?"

I got in on the passenger side and fastened my seat belt. "Dude, stealing a car and giving it back doesn't make me a bad guy. And I did give it back. That means I borrow cars." I was really hoping he would drop it. He didn't.

"And what about the driver? And don't bother lying, you

know you suck at it."

He's right, too. I can't lie worth a crap. Even being immortal and bloodless didn't mean I could spin a solid lie while looking my best friend in the eye. "Fine. I left him asleep in the back seat behind a biker bar on Central Avenue. He might have felt a little out of place when he woke up, but he was safe."

"Asleep? Or drained?" He looked down and not at me. He was really pissed.

"Asleep. I didn't drain him." I wasn't lying. I wasn't going to tell him the whole truth unless he pulled it out of me with a wrecker, but I wasn't going to lie, either.

"But you did feed, didn't you? Don't even answer. I can see it in your face. You look healthier than you have in years. I know you fed on him."

I didn't know what he was talking about, so I flipped down the sun visor on my side and checked myself out in the mirror. He was right. I looked *good*. Well, good for me, anyway. I still had an unruly shock of brown hair hanging in my eyes, and I was still too skinny, but I was a lot less pale than I had been when I woke up that night, and my eyes no longer had the pale, lifeless look that I'd come to equate with my reflection.

Oh yeah, the mirror thing. It's got more to do with silver than with mirrors and souls. Cheap, crappy mirrors like in cars work fine because they don't use silver as a reflective element. Good mirrors sometimes do, and silver doesn't react well to vampires, therefore we don't show up. Same deal with film. Silver nitrate is one of the main developing chemicals, so we'll show up on video or a digital camera, but not on real film. So I could check myself in the car mirror, but not in the mirror in my house.

Flipping up the visor, I said, "You got me. I did feed on the guy, but I didn't drain him, and I didn't really even drink that much. But that's not why I look like this."

I wasn't sure I wanted to tell him about Lilith, and even if I did, I wasn't sure how. He got bent out of shape about me feeding on a human, which is kinda the point of being a vampire. Telling him I'd fed on an immortal hottie would not go over well.

"I was at Phil's. I ate there."

"At Phil's?" He had looked away again, staring long and hard at the road, which meant he was expecting the kind of answer that'd make him mad. I swear, sometimes this partnership is like being married. We fight all the time and neither one of us is getting laid.

"Phil offered. He made it clear that it would be viewed as a serious breach of protocol for me to decline."

"Since when do we care about demonic protocol?"

"Technically, Phil's a fallen angel, which is different from a demon. I think."

"You hope. So, who did you drink from this time?"

Wow, he was going heavy with the guilt trip. He was making it sound like I went around drinking from people willy-nilly. Wrong. I quit doing that years ago, after I got a really embarrassing rash. Bad blood might not kill you, but a vampire can get all sorts of nasty things from it, and some of them take a while for even vampire metabolism to get rid of.

That made me wonder how long the "Lilith effect" would last before I went back to my pasty self.

"Her name was Lilith, and the light's green." I really wanted him paying attention to the road and not to the name of my new acquaintance. I didn't often get what I wanted.

We've read the same comic books, so if I knew Lilith, I was pretty sure he would. And judging by the fact that he pulled into a Burger King parking lot and shut off the car, he did.

"*Lilith?* Like Adam's first wife Lilith? Like the original feminist Lilith? Lilith who was condemned to walk the earth forever spreading lust through the souls of all she touches while unable to ever feel true love?"

Clearly he'd read way more comic books than I had, because the lust stuff was news to me. I sank down as far as the car seat would let me before I answered. "I guess that would be an accurate description."

Greg fumed. I didn't know fuming was audible but Greg managed to fill the car with the sound of it.

He took a deep breath, held it for a long time, let it out very slowly, and counted to twenty. In four languages. Four languages wasn't too bad. Greg was fluent in seven. Anything under five meant he was only moderately pissed. I thought I was maybe going to get out of this relatively unscathed.

"Well?" he finally asked.

"Well what?"

"Was it good?" There was a little longing in his voice, and I hoped that he might finally admit that he missed the taste of live blood.

"Dude, you have no idea. It made me tingle in places I'd forgotten I had places. I saw colors that I don't even have names for. I felt like I could run a marathon at noon in Arizona and not get the least bit crispy. It was amazing." I could have gone on describing the feeling of feeding on Lilith, but the look on Greg's face stopped me. "What's wrong?"

"Listen to me, and listen very carefully." He was scared. "You can never feed from her again. No matter what, no matter who it insults. Legend has it that her kiss, her very touch is so addictive that archbishops have burned their Bibles for a drop of her sweat. You have to stay away from her, or she could take you over completely. And a vampire under the control of a creature like Lilith would not make a pretty picture."

He was right. I didn't use much of my vamp powers in everynight life, but if Lilith was bad juju like Greg thought, then she could wreak some serious havoc if I fell under her control. And Greg was by far the better judge of character between the two of us. I trusted his opinion way more than my own.

"Fine, fine, I'll stay clear of her. You know how I hate going to Phil's anyway. Let's get out of here before some cop rolls up and decides we're making out in the BK parking lot."

"Well was it worth it?" Greg asked quietly.

"What? The blood? It was—"

"No." He cut me off sharply. "Did you get any useful information out of Phil?"

"Kinda. Apparently there's a Big Bad coming to town and if we don't stop it the world might end. Or something like that." I stared out the window, watching the billboards on I-485 roll past and thinking about Lilith. That chick scared me.

"Isn't that on the list of things you should *start* the conversation with?"

"Gimme a break. So I buried the lead. I saw Phil, I drank from an inappropriate woman, and there's a magic something-or-other coming that will destroy the world if we don't stop it. And how was your night, honey?" I kept looking out the window, but all I could see was a scared little girl and a shattered father that desperately wanted to see his child again.

"I hate you sometimes."

Chapter 14

"So, what's the plan?" Greg asked the second we got back into our apartment.

"I'm still working on that." I admitted, flopping down onto the couch and grabbing the Xbox controller. Hoping to distract him, I tossed him the other controller. "Madden?"

"Sure. I always think better with a little break. Did Phil give you anything we could use?"

I started up the game and picked my team. I always pick the Carolina Panthers, no matter how they did that season. I'm a hometown fan, what can I say? And besides, as long as they have Steve Smith, they'll always make for a fun video game. "He said that Halloween was the big day, that whatever we were up against had to be stopped by then, or not at all."

Greg stared at me with his mouth open while I sacked his virtual quarterback, forced a virtual fumble and sent a virtual Jon Beason to the end zone for a virtual touchdown dance. "You do realize Halloween is this weekend, right?"

"Yeah, I have a pretty good handle on the calendar."

"So what the hell are we doing playing video games?" Greg tossed his control at me and headed over to the computer.

"Really, dude? You don't want to play Madden but you'll go play World of Warcraft?" I was giving him a hard time, but sometimes I did it just because it was easy.

"Bite me. I'm checking email."

"No thanks, I've had my fill of supernatural Scooby Snacks tonight."

He flipped me off, then waved me over to the desk. "Come here, dude. You gotta see this!"

He was actually bouncing up and down in his chair. I thought we'd broken him of that habit in high school, but obviously not. I leaned over the back of his chair, as much to rescue the furniture from the shock load as anything else.

"What is it, bro?"

"I emailed the guys about the kidnappings to see what they knew, and they've got all the police reports!"

Oh. Crap. "The guys" were a trio of losers that worked in the biggest comic shop in town. They were understandably all over Greg for information on his "ongoing cases" whenever he went in to grab his subscriptions. Every once in a while we used them for daytime legwork or computer help when it was something we couldn't get Dad to do or if the computing was out of Greg's league. They were occasionally useful, but I always had a hard time balancing their annoying tics against the value of their assistance.

"Really? You emailed the Dork Brigade about this case?"

"Man, don't call them that. They're good guys. And Jason hacked into the police database and got us the police reports. So the guys are useful, too."

"And how many free comic books did you get for letting them help?" When he wouldn't answer me, I knew I'd hit home. My partner—the closet Spider-Man junkie.

"Do you want the reports or not?"

I did, so I shut up.

There were ten files, and the girl we'd exorcised the night before was slated to have been number eleven, so we added notes on her and Tommy into the mix and tried to see what patterns emerged. After three hours of taking apart class schedules, church attendance, club memberships and even school bus routes, I lost my patience.

"There's nothing here!" I lay on my back on the floor, surrounded by paper. I looked like I'd been mugged by a shedding yeti, and we had no more ideas than when we started. "What time is it?"

"Seven," he mumbled, still going over attendance records for the fifth victim.

"I'm going to bed. It's been a long night."

I stretched as I stood up, and my thighs threatened to

revolt. Vampire or not, you sit cross-legged on the floor for a few hours and even your butt falls asleep. I staggered off to my bedroom and crashed for a few hours while Greg kept going. He's always been better at homework than me.

We do sleep. And we dream, and we don't "die" every morning at sunrise. We can sense the sunrise. It's kinda like our bodies' way of warning us not to go outside for fear of becoming a pile of ash, but I've been known to pull an all-nighter (or in my case an all-dayer, I guess) when I needed to.

Today's sleep wasn't restful, not with visions of scared children running from sexy fallen angels dancing through my head. I got about six hours of fitful sleep and staggered out to the den to find Greg facedown in the scattered mass of case files.

I stepped over him as quietly as I could, opened the fridge and grabbed a bottle of orange juice. I didn't bother getting a glass, just sat on the couch in my boxers and drank straight from the plastic jug. We can drink, too, anything we want. No food, though. The digestive system stops working except for a liquid diet right after we wake up. We don't get any nutrients out of anything we drink except blood, but alcohol still works, only to a lesser degree.

So, I guess that answers Tommy's question about vampire poop. We don't poop, but if we play our cards right, we can pee in some spectacular colors, because what comes in, goes right back out again. You don't want to know how we found this out. Suffice to say that we were young and learning about our new abilities, and leave it at that.

"I don't care if we're dead, that's still gross." Greg's voice came from right behind me, and I jumped sky-high, spilling cold OJ on my lap. That's one of his favorite tricks, but it usually doesn't work on me, what with super-hearing and all. I'd been so wrapped up in the case that I didn't even hear him get up from the desk.

"I might be gross, but you're a dick," I said, looking around for something to dry off with. I gave up on the idea of finding anything lying around the den when I remembered that, yesterday, Greg had been home alone all night, which always led to an almost neurotic level of cleaning. I went into my room and got some fresh boxers and the rest of my clothes.

Greg was sitting up on the floor when I made it back to the den, a look of smug superiority on his face. "What?" I asked.

"What, what?" He kept grinning at me.

"Why are you sitting there grinning like the AV club president who bugged the girls' dressing room?"

"I *am* the AV club president who bugged the girls' dressing room," he reminded me without a hint of embarrassment.

"I remember. And you had that same stupid grin on your face then."

"Well I think I may have found our link between the victims. Career Day." He waved a piece of paper over his head like it was a checkered flag and he was an off-duty Daytona stripper.

I snatched the paper from him and looked at it. There was a column of initials, a column of dates and a column of school names. The school names I recognized, and it didn't take long to figure out that the initials and dates matched up with missing kids.

"Greg, there are only seven names here." I pointed to the paper.

"Yeah?"

"There were eleven victims, dude."

"Yeah, but seven of these schools had a Career Day the week before the kidnappings occurred. There's no way that's not statistically significant."

He had a point. "We need to look into it further."

"Really?"

"Yeah, I think it's a good idea."

Greg looked so happy that I wasn't dismissing his idea out of hand that you'd have thought I gave him an ice cream cone, or a puppy. Or a puppy with ice cream on it.

"Cool. Now what? Where do we start?" Greg asked. He headed to the coat closet and started gearing up—putting on his utility belt, boots, and other combat equipment. I stopped him before he got too far along.

"We start right here. At least until dark, bro. Remember, it's like two in the afternoon."

"Oh yeah. I just got so excited at having a real lead."

"I know, I know," I led him back over to the couch.

"Wanna play *Halo*?" I sat down with the game controller in one hand and my OJ in the other.

"Nah. If we can't go thwart evil, I'm gonna take a nap." My grumpy roommate then tromped off to his room for some shut-eye while I valiantly tried to save the world. Again.

Chapter 15

I finished off season two of *Dexter* on Netflix before Greg woke up. Not long after sunset, I heard the shower come on and a few minutes later, my partner emerged. He was dressed in all black, again, with his combat boots laced tight and his utility belt snug around his ballooning waist. I feel for Greg sometimes. I mean, who knew that turning into vampires wouldn't change our bodies into perfect examples of studliness, and we'd be trapped forever as the dorks we were on the last night of our lives?

The first thing we looked forward to when we got over the shock of being vampires was that now we could exercise all we wanted and build ourselves the buff bodies we'd never had in life. The first thing we realized after that was that no matter how much we exercised, our bodies were never going to change. This was not a welcome realization for either my pudgy best friend or me.

"Really, man. Do you have to wear the utility belt?" I laced up my sneakers and shrugged into my shoulder holster on the way out the door. I hid the firepower under a leather jacket before as we climbed the last steps and walked out into the cemetery.

We opened a tool shed that was really a two-car garage and hopped in Greg's car, a 1967 GTO convertible—black, of course. I always gave Greg a load of crap about his less-than-inconspicuous ride, but he'd had a man-crush on that car since we were alive, so no amount of teasing was going to get him to drive anything else. Besides, I had a blue Camry for when we needed to blend in.

"Where are we headed?" Greg asked as I got into the car.

I pulled out the file folder with all his Career Day notes and started to flip through it. It had been easy to find when he went to bed, because he'd written "CAREER DAY CLUES" on the outside of the folder in purple Sharpie. Sometimes I really thought my partner was secretly an illiterate twelve-year-old girl. I wouldn't have been too surprised to find his notes in a Trapper Keeper covered in unicorn stickers.

"There were three companies that had a table at every event. Bank of America, Joe's World of Tires and the Police Department. Bank of America makes sense, since their corporate headquarters is here. The owner of Joe's World of Tires is on the school board, and I think the cops were just looking for middle-school weed. But we should check them all out regardless."

"Why do we need to check out the cops? They're investigating the crimes. You don't think a cop could have done it, do you?"

My partner has a simple view of the world—police and firemen are good, and bad guys have twirly mustaches and bad French accents. It's charming, really.

"I don't think a cop abducted the kids, but it's possible. Cops are people, so they're suspects. We've got to look at everybody, bro."

"All right, but I don't think it's the cops."

I didn't either, but I could hope. A cop would be easier. I didn't think we were going to find our kidnapper anywhere in this list of companies. I didn't think our bad guy was still capable of "normal." It didn't feel right, if you know what I mean.

"So, where to first?" Greg gingerly backed the car out of the garage. I'm always amazed that he can be incredibly careful with his car but such a spaz on two feet.

"I think we start with the path of least resistance—Joe Arthur, owner of Joe's World of Tires and school board member. We should be able to play the PI card and find out who was representing the World of Tires at the Career Days straight from the source."

I gave him the address, and we headed out to meet the Tire King. I looked out the window and watched the city roll by. A flashing sign for the Morris Costumes Haunted House had me thinking a lot more than I wanted to about ten missing children and the fact that we only had a couple of nights left to stop something from coming to town that even a fallen angel was scared of.

It took us about half an hour to get to Joe Arthur's house, a modest ranch in one of the newer developments out past the university. These little subdivisions popped up all over Charlotte in the late 1990s as the banking boom hit, but now there was a For Sale sign in about every fourth yard.

I noted the bicycle lying beside the driveway. "Looks like Joe's got a kid right in the target age range," I whispered as we walked up to the front door.

"Yep. How do you want to play this? Good cop/bad cop? Two bad cops? Fangs out? Subtle?" He was bouncing up and down on the balls of his feet and shadowboxing his way up to the door. I grabbed the back of his utility belt and dragged him down the steps back to where I stood.

"I thought we'd ask him very nicely to invite us in, then see what he knows about the disappearances." I spoke very low and very slowly, and held one hand on Greg's shoulder to steady him while I tried to rein in his excitement. When you pair his enthusiasm with the fact that we haven't aged in fifteen years, it's easy to forget that he remembers the Reagan administration.

He deflated a little. "Oh."

I shouldered my way past him up the steps, and rang the bell. No one answered, so I rang again. I could hear people walking around inside, but when they didn't respond to the second ring, I knocked on the door. After a couple more minutes, a light flipped on over my head, and the door cracked open.

"Can I help you?" A sliver of a middle-aged woman's face appeared between the door and the jamb, as she looked at me through the security chain. The last time a woman was this unhappy to see me had been my date for the senior prom.

The woman's face was pinched, like she'd been a beautiful girl whose life hadn't worked out as well as she'd hoped, and her eyes darted along the street past me looking for something. I couldn't tell if she was more annoyed at me interrupting her evening, or worried about whatever might be out on the sidewalk at night. I'd seen that look before, on the face of my own mother, and it dredged up some memories that I didn't particularly enjoy.

"Is Mr. Arthur home?" I asked, reaching into my coat pocket for my investigator's license.

"No, he's not," she said, and moved to close the door in my face. I put a hand on the door and held it open. I couldn't go through without an invitation, but I could make sure she didn't close it completely, either.

I held my credentials where she could see them and said, "We're investigating the disappearance of some children. Maybe you've heard about the situation?"

"Yes, yes, I've heard of that. Awful stuff. But I don't see what that has to do with Joe. He's never really hurt anybody." She stopped, eyes round as she realized what she'd implied.

I began to doubt her certainty that Mr. Arthur was harmless. Maybe Greg had found something after all.

"We understand that, ma'am. We're hoping that he could answer a few questions for us about the Career Day events that he attended at several of the schools prior to the disappearances. He may have seen something that could be useful in our investigation. Could we come in and wait for him?" She looked increasingly nervous, and I suddenly became aware of another heartbeat in the house.

"Um... no, I'm sorry. I'm alone here, you see, and it wouldn't be proper. You understand? You're welcome to come back later, when my husband is home. Maybe tomorrow afternoon?"

I could hear the heartbeat moving closer to the door but I had no way in without an invitation. A wife-beater or a stone-cold killer could be behind that door, and I still couldn't do anything about it if I couldn't figure out how to get inside. I'm not sure how long I would have stood there if Greg hadn't pulled on my sleeve.

"Come on, James. We'll come back and visit when Mr.

Arthur is home. Thanks for your time, ma'am." He led me down the steps by my elbow and steered me toward the car.

"Dude!" I whispered. "What the hell was that about? Something had her wound up—her pulse was up, her skin was flushed, and there was definitely somebody else in that house. I could hear a man's pulse, racing. He was pretty excited, too." I put my elbows on the roof of the car and looked over at where Greg stood by the driver's door.

Usually he was the first one to leap into Super Hero mode. Now, he stood there quietly. I didn't understand. "Why aren't we doing everything we can to get her to let us in so we can help her?"

"Because I don't think she would appreciate our help," he said, with what I guess he meant to be a meaningful glance.

"What are you talking about?" I demanded.

"Let's see—skin flushed, heart racing, doesn't want us in the house, husband not home, someone else in the house with her. Even the man with a thousand strikeouts like you should be able to put those clues together." He smirked at me as realization dawned, and we got in the car.

"I get it." I closed the door. "She's having an affair, and her boyfriend was there. But where does that leave us with the Tire King?"

"Headed to Lucky Strike." Greg put the car in gear and headed towards the big outlet mall north of town.

"Why do you have a sudden urge to go bowling in the middle of an investigation?" Greg didn't really baffle me that often, but this time he had me flummoxed. Admittedly, he often baffled me, but it was usually with his staggering ineptitude with women. I can't understand how anyone can be immortal, live through all these years looking like he's in his twenties, and still have no more game than the dorky kids we were when we were turned.

"While you were trying to get the Real Housewife of Charlotte to let us interrupt date night, I was peeking through the kitchen window checking out the calendar on the fridge. Tonight is Joe Arthur's league night, so he'll be bowling for at least another couple of hours. All we need to do is grab him when he heads for his car, interrogate him, maybe munch on him a little, and find out what he knows."

"*Munch?* Did you, the closest thing to a vegan vampire I've ever met, just suggest that we actually feed from a suspect? Who are you and what did you do with Greg Knightwood?"

"I just thought that, you know, since you were off the wagon, bro, you might want another excuse to behave like an animal."

Now that made more sense. Ticked me off, but made sense. He just wanted to make me feel like a monster again. Whatever. I *am* a monster. And monsters eat. It's what we do.

"No, I think we can do without snacking on the suspects for tonight at least." I leaned back in my seat and contemplated staking my partner while he pulled into the mall's gargantuan parking lot. I couldn't stake him, but I could needle him. "Besides, I'm still full from yesterday."

"Well, if you're sure . . ."

"I'm sure. Park the car."

Lucky Strike is in Concord Mills, the gigantic mall north of town by the speedway. I've never gotten the hang of navigating that place. It's over a mile to walk the entire inside of it, and the mere concept of trying to drive through the parking lot always gives me the heebie-jeebies. Greg pulled up in front of the bowling alley, and we headed in. It made sense that the Tire King would bowl there. It was the closest alley to his neighborhood, and it had a truly excellent beer selection.

"Assuming he's here, do you really want to grab him as he exits?" I asked.

"Nah, I thought we'd flash our badges, ask a few questions about his whereabouts, hint around that his wife is having him investigated for infidelity, and all around ruin his night."

"That sounds a little extreme, doesn't it?" I asked. I liked it, but I wanted Greg to tell me that he'd seen what I saw in the wife's eyes.

"Were you not paying attention back there? That woman had all the classic signs of abuse to go with her affair. If the Tire

King's never used her for a punching bag, I'll eat your hat."

Bingo. We were on the same page after all. I knew from the look in her eyes that the wife had been slapped around more than once. If we could get a little payback on Mr. Joe Arthur, upstanding businessman and school board member, I was down with that.

"Fine, but we don't talk about his wife's boy toy unless he's really irritating."

"Nah, if he's really irritating we eat him. We ruin his marriage just for looking at me funny."

"You're wearing a utility belt. Everyone looks at you funny."

"Point," Greg agreed. "All right, we only ruin his marriage if we get something out of it."

"Deal. I'll lead."

"Why do you always lead?"

"I'm taller."

By now we had made it through the parking lot, down the mall and most of the way across the bowling alley, and I recognized Joe Arthur from his commercials. The Tire King was carrying a spare or two of his own, and I don't mean the bowling kind. He was a sixty-something Italian guy with more hair coming out of his ears than he had left on his head. He was about five foot eight which gave me a serious height advantage. I'm a couple inches over six feet. Even Greg had a couple inches on the Rubber Royalty.

He and his league buddies had the least flattering bowling shirts I'd ever seen. I've never met any guy over fifty (and over two-fifty) who can pull off horizontal stripes in turquoise, and these guys were no exception. I wondered if they realized they looked like turquoise Michelin Men.

We waited until Big Joe, as was embroidered on his bowling shirt, got up to bowl. Right in the middle of his backswing, I called out in my loudest voice, "Joe Arthur?" Since I was only about four feet from him, he jumped like a startled, overweight cat and threw a perfect gutter ball.

"Jesus Christ!" He stomped over to me and got as much in

my face as he could from his height and bellowed, "What the holy crap do you think you're doing? This is a league game! We're in the running for the championship! What kind of crap was that?"

If the garlic myth had been anything more than urban legend, Joe's breath would have put me down for the count. While my eyes watered, I flashed my badge. "Mr. Arthur, we have a few questions to ask you about some missing children."

The whole trick to flashing a fake badge is to control the flash. You have to open and close the wallet before anyone can get a good look at the contents. I'd actually practiced in front of a mirror when we first opened up shop as detectives. It's embarrassing to admit, but less embarrassing than how I learned to draw from a shoulder holster. Practice paid off, like now. His teammates were nudging each other as if to say, "Look at that. Joe's gone and got himself in trouble." They were focused on Joe, not questioning my ID.

"Mr. Arthur, is there somewhere we could talk?"

"I don't know anything about any missing kids. And I don't feel like talking to you. If you want to talk to me, talk to my lawyer first. And he'll tell you I don't know anything about any missing kids and don't feel like talking to you. Right, Mason?" He pointed over to a scrawny, balding man drinking beer from a plastic cup at a table near their lane. The man, who I assumed was Arthur's lawyer given Arthur's smirk, nodded like his head was spring-loaded and started over to us.

"Now that you've heard from my lawyer, get out of my face and let me finish my game." He turned back to the ball return machine, but I grabbed his wrist and turned him back to face me.

"I asked nicely first, Mr. Arthur. If I have to ask again, it won't be nicely." I spoke very slowly and kept my voice low. I didn't need his buddies seeing me threaten him and wondering what kind of cop would do that. That wouldn't end well for anyone, especially if anyone on the team got suspicious and grew a pair all of a sudden. Arthur looked into my eyes, and I put just enough mojo in them to show him I was not screwing around.

"Now," I told him, "bowl this ball and then come meet us at that table." I gestured to where Greg had settled in at a round plastic table with a pitcher of cheap beer and four plastic cups. "Bring your lawyer if you need to." I let go of his wrist and went over to the table with Greg.

Mason beat his client over to our table and began issuing a list of demands in a nasal, demanding tone that probably had Greg rethinking his stance against drinking from annoying humans. That was my criteria. Since I find pretty much everyone annoying, I drink from whoever I want to. Greg doesn't realize that my list of annoying people is about six billion names longer than his.

At the moment, Mason was top of the list. If I couldn't eat him, then he had to go. I leaned forward looked straight into his eyes and said, "Go to the men's room. Sit in a stall. Fall asleep for two hours. Then go do that thing you've always wanted to do but have been afraid would be too embarrassing."

Mason got up with a decidedly glassy look in his eyes and headed for the crapper.

I leaned back in my chair. "Well, that's one nuisance taken care of."

"You're evil. What do you think he'll do?" Greg asked.

"I don't even want to think about it. But I wouldn't be surprised if it involved anything from playing naked in the pond at Freedom Park to scaling the outside of the Bank of America building."

Joe Arthur, the Tire King himself, joined us at our table after picking up the spare. "Where's Mason?" he asked.

"He went to the can. Something about an upset stomach," I replied. Greg snorted a little beer out of his nose, and I kicked him under the table.

"Fine. You've got me alone. What's this about?" Arthur asked, obviously a man used to being in charge.

I decided to put an end to that as quickly as possible. I reached into the briefcase Greg had brought in from the car and brought out a stack of photographs. Smiling faces began to litter the table in front of us, some of the pictures curling a little as they soaked up spilled beer on the table. I didn't care. I wanted to watch Arthur's face as he realized who these children were. Ten pictures—school pictures, family vacation shots, all pictures of happy kids, beaming into the camera.

"Do you know who these kids are, Mr. Arthur?" I leaned forward, forcing his attention away from the photos and to my eyes. He looked up and I could see that he was shaken. There was something going on with this guy, and I needed to know what it was. He didn't smell like malice, more like mischief, but he was involved in something somehow.

"These are the kids that have gone missing. But I don't know anything about—"

I cut him off before he could go any further. "I know that, Mr. Arthur. You're not a suspect in these disappearances. But you were at seven of these children's schools in the days shortly before they went missing. You were there for Career Day, right?"

"Not all of them. Some of those Career Day things I sent Jake instead."

"Jake?" Greg sat forward. We hadn't heard anything about a Jake before now. "Who's Jake?"

"Jake's the manager of my Pineville store. I sent him to the schools on the south side of town, 'cause they're closer to him. But what's this got to do with me? I don't know anything about any of this stuff."

But he did—I could see it in his eyes, and more importantly, I could smell the little sweat that comes with fear. After a while you figure out what different kinds of fear smell like. For example, innocent oh-crap-I'm-about-to-get-eaten-by-a-vampire fear smells completely different than guilty as sin yeah-I-really-raised-a-super-demon-and-I'm-lying-out-my-butt-about-it fear. Joe's fear was somewhere between I-cheated-on-my-taxes fear and I've-got-corpses-buried-under-my-tomato-plants fear.

I turned the fear smell inside out, but I couldn't quite put my finger on the cause. I was so busy playing "Name That Fear" that I didn't sense a disturbance in the force until I heard Greg whisper "Oh, crap."

Chapter 16

Okay, fine, you got me. I didn't sense a disturbance in the force. But I did notice a silence fall over the bowling alley and smell a wave of fear rippling out from the main entrance. I looked over at the front door and saw the female detective from the night before talking to the shoe rental guy. He pointed to where we were sitting with the Tire King, and she started our way.

"Looks like we might have to come back to this conversation later, Mr. Arthur," I said, getting to my feet and looking for another exit.

"Where do you think you're going?" Arthur asked, getting up himself and blocking my escape route. "You can't come in here and make all these accusations then go running out on me. You sit your skinny ass right back down here and tell me what you think I have to do with those missing kids!"

I leaned down to the Tire King's face, which had gone an interesting splotchy purple color. I looked in his eyes and said, "Sleep."

He passed out cold and fell face-first onto the table, crushing his plastic cup full of Miller with his forehead. I turned him to the side to make sure he wouldn't drown in cheap beer and tried to formulate a plan.

"What are we gonna do?" Greg asked.

"I was really hoping you'd have a plan." My mind worked as fast as it could, which really isn't that fast, all things considered.

"I never have a plan. At least, not one you like."

He had a point there. Greg's plans usually involved some expensive piece of equipment that only existed in comic books, or so many plot twists that by the time he finished explaining the plan, I'd already punched somebody.

"Well, there's a first time for everything. But obviously

tonight ain't it." I stood up as the detective got to our table.

The look on her face dispelled any lingering hope that she hadn't noticed me looking out Tommy's hospital-room window. She was tall, and she'd pulled her curly hair back in a severe ponytail. Her blazer was pulled back to reveal an impressive rack, but my attention was drawn to her Smith & Wesson .40 pistol in a shoulder rig. I'll admit it, I have a bit of a thing for women who pack heavier ammo than me.

She snapped her fingers in front of my face and brought me straight out of my happy place and back to the beer-soaked bowling alley. "This would be an excellent time for you to explain to me who you are and why you keep showing up around my investigation."

The look on her face said she was a woman who brooked no BS, but I never let that stop me.

"I'm sorry," I said, holding out my hand and dropping into the hick accent I grew up with. "I think you must have me mistaken for somebody else. I'm Jimmy Black, assistant manager at the Monroe location of Joe's World of Tires. Can I help you with . . . something?" I put a little sleazy twist in there and ogled her chest, trying to make myself look like a slimy tire salesman.

Ogling her chest was not hard to do. More like a job perk.

"Really?" She said, and raised one eyebrow as if she knew something I didn't. "There is no Monroe location of Joe's World of Tires, and you're no more a tire salesman than I am a private investigator. Why don't you cut the crap, Mr. Black and tell me what you and your little friend here are doing screwing up my investigation before I haul you both downtown and book you on obstruction of justice charges."

I knew going legit and getting PI licenses would come back to bite me in the ass. And the irony of that concept is not lost on me. Having failed so miserably with Plan A, I skipped the as-yet-undeveloped Plan B and went straight for the mojo. I looked her in the eyes, which was surprisingly easy since she was almost my height, and said, "These are not the droids you're looking for. Move along."

"Are you on drugs?"

I looked over at Greg, who was as flabbergasted as I was. Mojo didn't fail. This was entirely unexpected. Surprise didn't help me process or communicate. "Huh?"

"You are on drugs. Great, just great. Not only do I have a PI sticking his nose in my case, I have a stoner PI sticking his nose in my case. Get up. You two are coming with me."

I looked at her again, and got serious with the mojo, really tried to supplant her will with mine. "No, we're not. You will leave here and forget you ever saw us. You came in, Joe Arthur was passed out drunk, he has nothing to do with these disappearances and you left. That is all."

She looked back at me just as hard and said "You are a pain in my butt, and you are going to jail for interfering with my investigation."

Since my vampire willpower wasn't working, Greg stepped in for the save. "Sorry to disappoint, but we're not going anywhere with you. I'm sorry we've run into this misunderstanding, but it's not going to happen. Now why don't you get in your car, go back to the station, and forget you ever ran into us this evening."

Greg's best mojo netted equally disappointing results and a disgusted headshake from the officer.

Both of us were seeing this cop in a whole new light. I'd never run into anyone who could shrug off multiple vamp mojo attempts, but this chick evidently had a will of cast iron.

She reached around to her belt and grabbed a radio, clicking it on as she brought it to her lips. "This is Detective Law. I need a wagon at Lucky Strike for two passengers." She put the radio back on her belt and looked at us. "You two are going to spend the night in a holding cell while I figure out exactly what I'm going to charge you with. Unless you have a really good story and start sharing it with me right now."

"Um... we were hired by the family of one of the kidnapped girls?" I offered up.

"The Reynolds family?" she asked.

I nodded.

"No, you weren't. They called me as soon as you left there.

I left instructions with every family to call me as soon as the vultures, and that means you, started coming around, so that I could run you off. So you came around, they called, and voilà! Here I am, running you off."

"But . . . but . . . ," I spluttered. I'm not proud of it, but splutter was the best I could come up with.

"But how did I find you? Mrs. Arthur also called me, and told me that you had just left her house, and were probably headed here to harass her husband publicly. Looks like she has some shred of marital loyalty left. And here we are."

"And here we are," I muttered. Here I was in the middle of a brightly lit public space with a human that I couldn't put the whammy on.

This was so far outside the norm, I was totally stumped. Greg and I had been bespelling humans for fun and foodstuffs for the better part of two decades, and nothing like this had ever happened before. Primitive survival instincts kicked in. We shared a look that said, "You wanna hit her or you want me to?" and I had just decided to deck the pretty detective in front of about seventy witnesses when her cell phone rang.

She pulled out her phone and pressed a button. "Law"

Thanks to our super-duper hearing, Greg and I had the benefit of following both sides of the conversation.

A disembodied voice said, "Detective, we have another abduction. Marjorie Ryan was last seen leaving a school dance with three of her friends forty-five minutes ago. Her friends all arrived home, but Marjorie did not. We've established a perimeter between the school and the home, and we have a chopper in the air. What's your twenty?"

"Lucky Strike bowling alley. I was about to question a potential suspect. Obviously, he's not our guy. I'm on my way, should be there in fifteen."

I held up my hands and started to back away, saying, "You've obviously got a lot going on, so we'll get out of your way. Good luck catching the bad guys!"

"Don't even think about moving. As a matter of fact, you two are still going downtown, if for nothing else than to keep you out of my hair. No way do I need you mucking around my crime scene and getting in my way. Gimme your right hands." She reached behind her and grabbed a pair of handcuffs.

I shook my head. "Look, Detective. You don't have enough to charge us with anything, and handcuffing us and leaving us here is a bad idea no matter whose police procedure manual you cite." I thought if mojo wasn't working then maybe I could appeal to her sense of reason. "If you think you need to keep an eye on us, take us along. My partner and I have a lot of experience in unusual cases. We could probably be helpful if you'd just let us."

"Okay, maybe you would be useful." She seemed to relent, and reached out to shake my hand. Without thinking, I took her hand, and just like in a thousand bad cop movies, she slapped a cuff on it. Then she reached over to the swivel chair mounted to the scoring station and locked the other cuff around it.

"Now stay put. You," she said to Greg, "give me your keys."

He reached in his pocket and handed her the keys to the Pontiac. "I'm gonna get those back, right?" he asked, looking like a whipped puppy.

"Sure. You can pick them up at the station downtown tomorrow morning. I'll be sure to have them there by nine." With that, she turned and headed for the door. I sat down with my arm twisted uncomfortably behind me and looked over at Greg, who took the other seat.

"This would be a very good time to tell me you have a spare set of car keys," I said, glaring at him.

"Under the back bumper, bro. No worries."

"Good, then I won't have to strangle you in your sleep."

"I don't breathe, so it wouldn't make any difference."

"It would make me feel better."

"Yeah, I can see where you might be a little disgusted with yourself for falling for the old handshake/handcuff switcheroo." He looked unbearably smug sitting there. I hate it when he's got the right answers for things. It messes with the natural order of the universe.

"So, how you planning on getting out of there?"

I stood up and stepped around behind the chair, hiding the handcuff from the rest of the bowling alley with my body. I twisted and pulled, but couldn't get enough leverage to get it off my arm. The cuff groaned a little. I shoved the metal band further up my forearm until it was nice and tight. I flexed one more time, but all I got for my trouble was a red mark around my arm and a couple of stares from a passing waitress.

"Did somebody forget to eat his Wheaties this morning?" Greg asked. "You should be able to snap that like a pretzel."

"Yeah, I know, but I can't get a good angle on the cuff. Time for Plan B." I reached down and grabbed the back of the chair with my free hand. I worked the molded plastic for a minute, couldn't get it to give at all, and finally just ripped the whole seat free of the swivel, which consisted of cheap metal fastenings. I stood there in the middle of the bowling alley with a chair hanging from one wrist. "Let's go," I snarled at Greg, who was having trouble getting to his feet because he was laughing so hard.

I trudged to the front door, pausing long enough to tell the counter guy that the chair in lane nine was busted, and dragged the stupid chair all the way out the mall entrance to the parking lot, attracting more than one strange look on the way. I got to the car and reached under the bumper. I felt around and pulled out one of those magnetic key boxes, and slid it open, only to find a business card for Detective Sabrina Law. She had written a note on the back of the card saying, "Hide it better next time."

Greg made it out to the parking lot in time to laugh some more at the sight of a gangly six-foot-three-inch vampire stomping around the lot cursing inventively and swinging a plastic chair around his head by a handcuff.

"Dude, hold still, let me get you out of that thing," he said when I stopped swearing and flailing.

He reached into a pocket of his utility belt and brought out a small folding saw, the kind they sell at sporting goods stores. I thought of about seventeen wisecracks, but decided I valued emancipation from the bowling alley furniture over a good zinger and held my tongue. His little saw was surprisingly effective, and in a couple of minutes, I was free.

Well, mostly free. I still had a handcuff dangling from my wrist, but there was no longer a giant hunk of molded plastic attached to it. Some nights you can only ask for so much, and this was shaping up to be one of those.

"I don't suppose you have another set of keys in that belt, do you?" I asked hopefully.

"No, but I have the next best thing," Greg replied.

Before I could ask what exactly that was, he reached under my arm, grabbed my Glock and walked over to where a young couple was doing what young couples do in the back lanes of parking lots. Greg tapped on the glass with the pistol, and then put his fist through the back passenger window. He pulled a skinny teenage kid out through the window, pointed the gun at his rapidly shriveling pride and joy, and hinted that the kid should run away. Then he leaned into the back window, smiled at the girl broadly enough to show a lot of fang, and laughed as she beat a hasty retreat out the other door. He tossed a T-shirt at her retreating, and naked, back, and reached into the floor of the backseat for the boy's pants.

"Subtle. That looked like something I would do," I said as I walked around and got into the passenger seat. Greg had retrieved the car keys from the boy's pants by then, settled himself behind the wheel and put the car in gear.

"Sorry," he said without an ounce of remorse. "I was under the impression that we were in a hurry. Problem solved."

He peeled rubber out of the parking lot and handed me back my gun. I tuned the radio to an oldies station and cranked some vintage Springsteen as we headed off to the site of the latest kidnapping. I wasn't sure what our detective friend would think about our appearing at her crime scene, but I wasn't too inclined to care. We only had about forty-eight hours to stop the summoning of a serious metaphysical beastie from taking place, and our Big Bad was now one ankle-biter closer to its quota.

Flying under the radar of the cops was no longer an option.

Chapter 17

Every cop in the greater Charlotte area was camped out in a three-block radius between the latest victim's school and home. It would have been a great time for bank heists, jewelry store capers or just knocking over liquor stores for pocket change.

Greg and I parked the car a couple of blocks outside the ring of flashing blue lights and left the keys in the ignition. I'd rifled through the kid's wallet on the way across town and found twenty-seven bucks and six condoms. The kid was something of an optimist. Or an overachiever.

We circled the perimeter until we found a young, scared-looking cop working a section of sidewalk alone. I walked up to him, smiling my friendliest smile, which is not much more reassuring than Hannibal Lecter after eating bad steak tartare, but I got close enough to see the color of his eyes.

"H-hold it right there," the kid stammered and put his hand on his gun. I hoped he wouldn't shoot himself in the foot before I mojo'd him. "You'll have to go around, sir. Sorry for any inconvenience."

"Me, too, Officer. Now give me your handcuff keys." His eyes went glassy and he reached around to the back of his belt and handed me the keys. I unlocked the cuff around my wrist, relieved to find that my mojo wasn't permanently on the fritz. It simply didn't work on one particular badass Amazon warrior princess cop.

"Thanks, Officer," Greg said politely. "You never saw us."

Then we split up. Greg headed towards the kid's home to see if he could pick up anything there because he's more sensitive to psychic garbage than I am. Psychic anything is right in his wheelhouse.

I concentrated on what I do best—looking for things to hit

and annoying pretty women. Toward that end, I headed toward the center of activity in hopes of finding Detective Law. I used her ever-so-helpful business card and my PI credentials to badge my way into the mobile command tent they had set up in the schoolyard, and tapped her on the shoulder.

"Lose these?" I dangled her handcuffs from one finger. The cops around us let out a couple of wolf whistles and I put on my best imitation of a rakish grin.

It probably worked a little, because she stepped in close to me, reclaimed her handcuffs, and whispered in my ear, "I don't know how you got loose, or how you got here, and I don't really care. But you've got about three seconds to get out of my crime scene before I shoot off something you're probably inordinately proud of."

I looked down and saw her Smith & Wesson pointed at Little Jimmy and stepped back quickly.

As much as I usually enjoy banter, we were on a deadline. "This is getting old. Why don't you take me outside?" I turned around and put my hands behind my back, making it easy for her to re-cuff me. I also made sure there was no furniture nearby.

"Oh, I will. Mostly because I don't want everybody to see me beat the crap out of you." She put a hand on my elbow and walked me out of the tent. As soon as we were in some relative shadow, I stopped walking. She had to stop, too, because, despite my skinny frame, she couldn't move me. She looked up, confused.

"You want to take these cuffs off me now," I said.

"I don't think so," she spat.

"It wasn't a question."

She got right up in my face and was about to say something that probably would have accomplished absolutely nothing when I dangled her cuffs in front of her face. It was worth petty larceny to see the look on her face. She got another look entirely as I crushed the handcuffs into a mangled mess of steel and dropped them at her feet.

"Don't bother trying that again." I kept my voice low, and my expression calm. I needed her, and whether she knew it or not, she needed me. She started to go for her gun, but I caught her hand as she was reaching for it. "Don't," I said. "You'll never make the draw, and it wouldn't matter if you did. You know that somewhere in the hindbrain that protects you. Now ignore all this—me, what I am—for a little while. Believe me when I say that if I'd wanted to kill you, I'd have done that already. All I want is to get this kid back home safely. You'll find that I'm happy to take orders, but we need to work together."

"Why should I believe you?" she asked.

"You've already checked us out. You know we weren't anywhere near the crime scenes. Right?"

To her credit, she didn't try to act like she hadn't followed up on us. "Yes. You're apparently just what you say you are—a couple of low-rent private eyes with no priors. That doesn't explain why I should let you in on a police investigation."

"Looking around this joint, I'd say you've pulled in every resource you can lay your hands on. I'd guess that you're about one missing kid away from calling in a pet psychic to interview the family schnauzer. Just call us consultants."

"I know *how* to get you on the case, asshole. What I don't have yet is a good reason *why* to put you on this case." She crossed her arms in front of her chest, and I looked back at her face, disappointed.

"Because we've proven that you can't get rid of us?" I asked hopefully.

"That may be true, but I don't have to enable you. Now I'm going to go interview the parents. Stay the hell away from them, and stay the hell away from my investigation. I can't keep you off public property, but if I catch you interfering in my investigation again, I can sure as hell put you in the county jail for obstruction of justice."

I stepped back. She stared at me for a minute, and if looks could kill, I'd have been dead all over again.

I looked at her for a long moment and finally nodded. "You win, Detective. We'll stay out of the way." I turned and headed toward the school.

"Hey," she called out after me. "Wait a minute." She took a couple of long strides over to me and leaned in close. "I don't know how you did that little handcuff trick, but it's gonna take a lot more than that to scare me. When I get done with this mess, I am going to find out what your deal is. And if I don't like what I find, you're going to be very unhappy for a very long time."

I looked at her for a minute. "I've been unhappy for longer than you can imagine. Without an end in sight." I turned around and walked off in the direction of the school to see what I could find about a missing little girl.

I kicked myself a little for letting her needle me into that parting shot. I'm not the brooding type, but something in her eyes made me miss being human, just for a minute. I've gone whole years without missing the sun, but right then the prospect of never being able to wake up next to a beautiful woman and watch the sunlight play across her back and legs was enough to make me ache.

I had been lost in my thoughts for a minute or two when I caught a strange scent on the air. I scanned the sidewalk ahead and pulled out my cell and called Greg.

"Yo. Where you at?" I asked.

"God, your grammar gets worse the longer you're dead. I'm on the roof of the school. I found something funny up here. Where are you?"

"About to hop the playground fence over by the swings. Are you where you can see me?"

"Yeah. And fortunately for you I'm the only one who can see you. The cops assigned to the school are all out front and inside. How'd your conversation with the hot cop go?"

"About like all my other conversations with beautiful women," I grumbled.

"That bad, huh? Well, come up here and take a look at this."

"I'll be up in a second." I crossed the playground, trying to figure out what the smell was. It wasn't quite sulfur, but it had a little of that acrid tang to it. I couldn't place where I had smelled it before, so I took a running leap onto the roof and walked over to where Greg was kneeling in front of what looked like a protective circle.

I'm no magician, but I've read a lot of comic books and I know a magic circle when I see one—as long as the circle is drawn by someone with a taste for 1970s Marvel comic villains. This one passed my very limited quality control.

Greg had dabbled in magic when we were in high school, so he had more actual knowledge of the mystical arts than I did. Of course, a retarded orangutan that has walked through a magic shop once has more knowledge of the mystical arts than me. Still, I felt qualified to make this call. "A protective circle?"

"No, it's wrong."

"Nope, pretty sure it's a circle, bro."

"Yes, I know that. But look at these symbols." He pointed to several scribbles and squiggles around the inside of the circle. "These should be on the outside of the circle, so that whatever was summoned into the circle couldn't scratch them out and alter the protection of the circle."

"What if you weren't trying to pull something into the circle?" I asked.

"What do you mean?" Greg looked at me with eyebrows raised.

"Well, couldn't you cast the circle around you, then do a summoning spell so that whatever you summoned couldn't get you before going off to wreak havoc? You'd be safe. It's probably not foolproof or exactly the safest thing in the world, but would it work?"

Greg's sat down on the roof with a *thud*. His eyes got big. "I hadn't even thought about that. That's so awful I didn't think anyone would consider it."

"I think someone did. You don't get eaten, and when you send the *whatever* back to *wherever* all you have to do is erase the circle, right?" I wasn't sure what I was missing, but it looked like it was going to be bad. I hate having smart friends.

"What's so bad about that? Really? You don't get it?" Greg replied. I mentioned I hate having smart friends, right?

He went on. "What's so bad is that once you summon a *whatever* from *wherever* without a circle to bind it, then that whatever is free to do whatever it likes to whoever it wants to do it to, without you being able to banish it to anywhere, much less to wherever it came from in the first place!"

"Not to be the king of understatement or anything, but that doesn't sound good," I said as Greg's explanation began to sink in.

"Yeah. If you hide in a circle and don't bind a demon, for example, into another circle, then that demon is just set . . . free. It can't get you, but it can do anything it wants and you don't have any control over it, except maybe where and when you summon it."

"The timing. The girls," I said in almost a whisper.

"Yeah, the girls," Greg agreed. "Whoever summoned the demon must have waited until they were the only ones left around, then cast the spell."

"But how would they know they were getting the right girl?" I asked.

"I don't think it mattered. I think the summoning party wanted to be sure the demon took an innocent. Which innocent it got was irrelevant."

"So some little—this little girl just drew the short straw?" Even with everything I'd seen, that didn't sit right with me.

"Pretty much." Greg sat there on the roof, looking at the circle and shaking his head. I reached out a hand and pulled him to his feet.

"Come on," I said, walking toward the edge of the roof.

"Wait a sec. I gotta blow this up first." He reached into his utility belt and sprinkled a white substance on the circle. A pale blue smoke hissed up from the roof, and the circle disappeared.

"What was that?" I asked.

"Salt. It's bad juju for magic stuff. Now this circle can't be used again."

"Good deal. Now let's get moving." I resumed walking to the edge of the roof.

"Where are we going?" He asked, falling into step beside me.

"Back to the playground. I smelled something funky, and

we might be able to trace this thing by the scent."

"Sometimes I think you only keep me around for my nose," he grumbled.

"And your car. But you've got a better nose than me, so I need you to take a whiff, tell me if it's important, and if it is, you need to track the whatever it is to wherever it went."

"All right, I'll play bloodhound, but if you try to put me in one of those stupid doggy Christmas sweaters again, I'm gonna stake you in your sleep."

Chapter 18

We circled around the playground a couple of times before I caught the scent again. I waved Greg over to where I had smelled it, and he took a deep breath. "Smell that?" I asked.

"Yeah, dude. Smells like vindaloo."

"Good. We know the kind of demon then."

"No, you magic-backward moron. Chicken vindaloo. It's an Indian dish with a lot of curry. Should be pretty easy to follow in this white-bread part of town." Greg took off toward the fence and I followed, trying not to lose him while still keeping an eye peeled for the cops.

Trailing the Big Bad was always so much easier when the Scooby gang on *Buffy* did the trailing. They rarely had cops crawling their turf. Of course, Buffy was usually trying to kill guys like us. I probably shouldn't enjoy the Whedonverse as much as I do.

We hopped the fence and followed the trail of Indian cuisine into a patch of woods separating the school from the neighborhood where Marjorie lived. Our vamp night vision is equal to any human's day sight. Unfortunately, our trail navigation skills were piss-poor. We went stumbling through the woods like a pair of drunken rhinos.

After about ten minutes, Greg held up one hand. Since I was looking at my feet and not at his hand, I walked into his back. Laid him out like a pin at the bowling alley.

"Dammit, Jimmy, would you watch where you're going?" He picked himself up off the ground and brushed twigs and leaves off his knees.

"I was watching where I was going, but I wasn't watching where you were stopping. So why are we stopping?" I helped him up, figuring it was the least I could do.

"I heard something. It sounded like someone trying to be stealthy in the woods."

"So it sounded nothing like us?"

"Not a thing like us. Now shut up and let me try to hear it again."

We heard the exact opposite of someone trying to be stealthy—several loud gunshots came from about a hundred yards in front of us. Greg and I looked at each other and then bolted toward the sound.

That's either brave or stupid for most people, but we aren't people and can't be killed by bullets, unless they manage to completely destroy our hearts or sever our heads. Since those kinds of bullets are pretty rare, running toward the sound of gunshots is generally worse for those doing the shooting than for us.

We hauled ass through the woods, managing to only trip on two or three exposed tree roots in the process, then drew up short at the edge of a clearing. Detective Law was in the clearing, apparently the source of the shots. I say "apparently" because she was no longer holding her gun, and from the looks of her, barely holding on to consciousness. She was lying on the ground in a circle of little girls. None of them looked older than nine, and they were beating the crap out of her.

You didn't have to be the sharpest knife in the drawer to figure out pretty quickly that these were not ordinary little girls. Even the village idiot would have guessed something was amiss when one of them picked Law up and threw her across the clearing at a huge tree. I nodded to Greg, and he jumped over to intercept the flying detective before her head became one with the splinters.

I stepped into the clearing, and tried to buy some time with my wits and humor. God only knew how that was going to go. If I was ever going to be universally funny, it was time for the comedy gene to kick into high gear.

"Now, girls, I don't like curfew any more than you do, but that's no reason to beat up a cop," I said, leaning against a pine tree in what I thought was a jaunty fashion. I felt far less jaunty when a bunch of little girls, all sporting glowing eyes à la *Children of the Corn*, turned to me and started walking in my direction.

I thought for a second about what it had taken to subdue the last one of these possessed super-brats and decided discretion was the better part of valor. I waited until the first couple of them were close enough to almost reach me, and then I jumped straight up into the tree. I cleared a good fifteen feet and swung up onto a branch, looking down to see the girls surrounding the base of the tree like little pigtailed bloodhounds.

"Greg, you got any brilliant ideas? Now would be the time to send 'em my way!" I yelled across the clearing.

"I was thinking 'run like hell' sounds like a plan," he shouted back.

"I don't think that is an option, gentlemen." The woman's voice came out of the darkness on the edge of the clearing. A middle-aged woman with her hair in a bun stepped into the circle of trees and said, "Come to me, my children."

The little girls with the creepy eyes formed a double rank in front of the woman and stood there, so silent that I couldn't tell if they were breathing, even with my heightened senses.

"Okay, lady. We don't have any quarrel with you. Let the kids go and we can all be on our merry way." I tried to hold my voice steady, and really hoped that my coat had enough drape in it to hide the fact that my knees were shaking to a marimba beat. Greg looked up at me from across the clearing and mouthed something at me, but even if I had been able to read lips, he was too far away for me to understand what he wanted.

Any hope of getting out of the woods without a serious fight, and probably a serious beating, went out the window when the bun-head opened her mouth again. "I don't think you're going anywhere, vampire. You got lucky the last time we met, but I don't see any automobiles around for you to hit me with tonight."

Crap. Just crap. In my experience anyone who felt comfortable delivering a monologue before the punching started was strong enough to wreck my day. Plus the middle-aged woman was clearly possessed by the demon that had gotten us into this mess in the first place.

I took stock of the situation from my elevated vantage point in the tree. I was facing a bunch of possessed little girls and what looked like one really pissed-off cafeteria lady. Greg was trying to help Detective Law to her feet, and I had no random automobiles to throw at the rug rats from hell.

I decided to try and talk my way out of trouble. It used to work with principals, so why not crazed cafeteria-lady demons? "What's the plan? You've gotten one step closer to your quota tonight, and then what? You turn in the box tops for an iPod?"

"Fool!" shouted the woman. "Do you have any idea the forces you are tampering with?"

"None whatsoever. Why don't you enlighten me." The longer I kept her talking, the better the chances Greg would think of something brilliant. I hoped. Boy, did I ever hope. I also hoped that this curry-scented psycho had seen all the same movies I had and knew her role was to provide a soliloquy on her plans and motives, giving me enough time to avoid being killed.

"Foolish vampire, the world as you know it is coming to an end. The reign of mankind is over. When I complete my ritual and bring my father forth, all will kneel before the Dark Lord, and Belial shall be favored among all the Host!"

I had no idea what the "Host" was, and the very sound of "Dark Lord" made me more than a little uncomfortable. And she was yelling. In my experience, supernatural bad guys yell right before they hit you very hard, or at least try to kill you in some unpleasant fashion. I thought I'd pre-empt her hitting me and take the fight to the bun-head.

I hopped down from the tree with a nice cape-billowing move and drew my weapons. With a pistol in one hand and a knife in the other I felt marginally better about my chances of surviving the next thirty seconds. All that good feeling evaporated when Detective Law spoke from behind me.

"Drop the gun, Black." I heard her chamber a round, and sighed.

"Greg, why is she pointing a gun at me?" I asked without

turning around.

"Because I don't like people threatening the possessed bodies of innocent little old ladies on my shift. Now drop the gun," Detective Law repeated.

"No," I said, never taking my eyes off the little old lady, who was the source of much greater concern than the cop with a gun pointed at my back.

"No?" She sounded surprised.

I suppose people don't typically decline when she points a weapon at them and orders them to disarm, but I didn't have a lot of time for verbal sparring. "No. Greg, get the nice police lady out of here before she gets killed." I raised my pistol and took aim at the bun-lady's head. "Last chance, Mrs. Butterworth. Let the kids go and I won't ventilate your forehead."

Bun-head wasn't impressed. "Your policewoman is right, you won't shoot an innocent body, and you still have too many of your idiotic human ideals."

I hate it when the bad guys have a good read on me. Maybe I should start wearing a mask.

"Children," the bun-lady demon called. "Kill them all." She waved one hand at the three of us, and the entire cast of *Annie* rushed us.

Chapter 19

Most nights I have qualms about hitting kids, but this wasn't one of those nights. I holstered my weapons and kicked the first brat all the way across the clearing, as gently as I possibly could. The second one to get within arm's reach ended up as a projectile, too. The two of them hit trees and slumped to the ground, momentarily stunned. That only left about eight attacking the three of us for the moment, but I had a sneaking suspicion that Detective Law wasn't going to be much use in this fight.

A glance behind me confirmed my suspicions, as several of the brats had her down on the ground and were beating the crap out of her. Again. I couldn't concentrate on her plight for long, though, because there were three of the little ankle-biters swarming me, and the two I'd incapacitated earlier didn't have the courtesy to stay down for long. As much as I hated it, the gloves were going to have to come off.

"I really hope you've got a good idea, bro!" I heard Greg yell from behind me, then I heard a loud *oof!* and a thud that let me know he was off his feet. I jumped back into my tree to get a second's breathing room, only to have company on my branch almost immediately.

"Not fair!" I yelled. "No fair chasing me when I'm trying to figure out how to kick your aaaaa—" I was trying to say something witty (and distracting) when the branch broke and dumped me and the kid who had jumped after me fifteen feet onto the forest floor. I could have been hurt if I'd landed wrong, but at the last minute I twisted and landed on the kid instead.

A remnant of morality twinged, but then I remembered that I *eat people*. It's not like I was interviewing to be her babysitter, and she started it by invading my tree. She puked a little from my having landed on her, and seeing that gave me an idea. It also made me a little nauseous.

I had to get free of the fray for a second to clear my mind. I picked the girl up by her ankles, and twirled in a circle, swinging her like a hammer toss in high-school track and field. After I'd leveled the three other kids surrounding me, I tossed her at the bun-demon and yelled over to Greg.

"Dude!"

"Yeah?" he croaked. He had a kid in each hand by the scruff of the neck, and one was on his back choking him with one hand and hitting him in the head with the other. I would have laughed if I hadn't seen four crumb-snatchers running back toward me full tilt.

"What was that crap earlier about salt breaking spells?"

"Salt—*urk*—disrupts the flow of magical energies. It'll break almost any spell." He managed to throw off all three kids for a second, but then two more dropped on him from a tree.

"Will it screw up stuff like summoning and possession?" I asked, jumping and weaving as the little girls closed on me once again. I needed to end this quick, before I killed a kid or before one of them decided that a broken branch would serve as a stake. Or beat the helpless detective to death.

"I think so!" The response came from under the pile of bodies where Greg was lying.

"This would be a good time for you to—*oof*—tell me you've got more in your utility belt!"

The whole pile of possessed bodies flexed, then flew apart as Greg jumped to his feet. The little rug rats immediately headed back at him, but Greg was ready. He reached into a pouch on his belt and tossed white powder into the faces of the girls attacking him, and they immediately slumped to the ground unconscious. Right at that moment I felt a tremendous pain behind my left knee, and looked down to see one of the brats had actually locked her teeth into my hamstring.

"Oh, that is it!" I bellowed. "Biting is my gig, you little urchin!" I snatched her off my leg and threw her over to Greg. "Salinate this little brat, please!"

"I don't think that's a word, Jimmy."

"I don't have time to call Webster's, man, just make with the salting!"

"Happy to help, bro," he called back.

A few minutes later we were panting in a clearing surrounded by eleven unconscious, salty little girls. Bun-Head was gone. She must have decided that discretion was the better part of whatever and hauled ass out of there once we started dispelling the kids. Apparently, all it took was a good dousing with sodium chloride to toss the demons out and turn them back into normal children.

It was probably going to take a lot more work to get Detective Law back to normal. She was sitting with her back to a tree and her gun in both hands. The slide was back and the gun was obviously empty, but that didn't stop her from pointing the weapon at us and dry firing frantically as we approached.

"*Shhhh* . . . it's okay. We're the good guys. We're not going to hurt you, I promise." I kept my voice low and slowly moved to sit down next to her. All I really had to work with was a little experience working with frightened animals, and reruns of *Dog Whisperer* on Animal Planet. I thought it might be a good idea to get down to her level and look as non-threatening as possible. That was a little tough, since I was fairly bloody. At least it was all my blood.

After a minute I reached out and very gently took the gun from her hand. She resisted for a second, but eventually let go, and I ejected the magazine and put the empty weapon in my coat pocket. "Are you all right?" I asked.

"I don't think so," she said very quietly.

"I'm not surprised. Most people need a little adjustment period the first time they experience something like this."

She looked over at me, and I could hear shock hovering on the outer edges of her voice. "The first time? Exactly how often does crap like this happen?"

"Unfortunately," Greg said as he slid down to sit on the other side of her, "this sort of thing happens all too often. And we've observed that once the barriers to belief are removed, that you may find yourself seeing more and more of it. You see, our society erects so many roadblocks to any understanding or analysis of the paranormal that it is almost impossible to truly investigate anything that happens outside the ordinary."

Greg had the bit between his teeth. This was his subject, and I didn't have the heart to deny him a good ramble. I'm sure he said a lot more, and I'm sure that it made perfect sense to anyone that would care, but I was most certainly not in that camp, so I did what I'd done for the past two decades whenever Greg started one of his rambles. I had a drink.

Lucky for me, my flask had made it through the fight without any major structural damage. I had a belt of Glenfiddich and passed it over to Detective Law. "Want a belt?"

She took the flask and turned it up for a long slug. "Nice. What is this?"

"Scotch. What were you doing in the woods?"

"The last girl to disappear had her cell phone turned on. I initiated a GPS trace and it led me here. But . . . what was all that?"

"That's a longer story than we have time for. You think you can stand?"

"Probably."

"Good, because we should be moving along before your comrades in arms show up."

"Why?" She looked around at the unconscious little girls scattered around the clearing. "We can't leave them lying here."

"If experience serves as any guide, and what good are the bruises if it doesn't, they'll be out for a couple more hours at least. Your people will find them." I got to my feet and brushed the worst of the dirt off my jeans and coat. I reached down and helped her to her feet and returned her sidearm to her. "We, on the other hand, have a different task. In case you hadn't noticed, we're still missing one grumpy old lady."

"Shit. Where did she go?" She put a fresh magazine into the pistol, chambered a round, and holstered her gun.

"If I knew that, I wouldn't be missing her. Now come on, we've gotta go after her, and we don't need to get tangled up in a bunch of—Well, crap, here comes the parade." All hope of getting out of the woods without a few hours of questions evaporated as the bulk of the Charlotte-Mecklenburg Police Department's SWAT team surrounded us, assault rifles at the ready. "I hope you have a foolproof plan for dealing with this."

"I do," she replied. She stepped forward, badge in hand, and yelled "Lower your weapons, boys! Stand down. We've got it under control."

One of the guys in body armor came over, and she huddled together with him for a few seconds. Whatever she was selling, he was buying, because in no time at all he had guys running back through the woods for stretchers and ambulances. Greg elbowed me and motioned to the cops. I gave him my best hell-if-I-know shrug, and we sat down at the base of a couple of huge oaks to wait. Looked like we were going to be stuck in the woods with the cops while our bun-headed magical psychopath got away. Again.

Chapter 20

"Well, Detective, do you believe me now when I say that we can be useful?" I asked as Greg, Detective Law and I sipped coffee at a small table the SWAT boys had set up.

"You've got your moments, I'll give you that. I haven't seen martial arts work like that in a long time, and I sure wouldn't have expected it from you two," she said.

That's a pretty standard coping mechanism for people who see us in action. There are so many kung fu movies out there. They just think we're super black belts or something. I usually don't bother to correct them. This was another one of those times.

"Do you think we can get a handle on some of that reward money?" I asked, as subtle as I knew how to be.

"Maybe. You were actually investigating, and you did help in recovering the kids, so I guess you're entitled." She looked disappointed somehow, and that bothered me a little.

"You know, it's not a big deal, I was just thinking—"

She cut me off with a wave of her hand "No, you're right. You guys deserve some recognition for the work you've done."

That set off an alarm bell or two. The last thing we wanted was recognition. Actually, the last thing we wanted was a nice summer vacation in Phoenix, but recognition from any authority was pretty low on our list of desires, too. Really, I just wanted a few bucks to get the new Madden NFL game. I was really tired of playing Brett Favre in a Packers jersey. While I was mentally kicking myself for opening my big mouth, she walked over to a black guy in a nice suit and gestured toward us.

Greg leaned over to me and asked, "What did you do?"

"Something stupid."

"What else is new? Would you care to be more specific?"

"I mentioned the reward."

"You're an idiot."

"I know. I think we should leave now before we have to fill out forms or answer questions."

"The first girl you talk to in fifteen years, and you run her off because you're a greedy shit. Well done."

"She is not the first girl I talked to. I talked to that girl at Phil's the other night."

"Okay, the first human girl that you weren't simultaneously chatting up and putting a dollar in her garter."

"Point to you. Now let's get out of here."

We double-checked to make sure Detective Law and her boss were looking the other way and slid off into the night. Greg's car was still at the bowling alley, and the keys were still in the pocket of a cop who was not in a mood to look kindly upon me. We improvised and mojo'd a cop into giving us a ride. He pulled up in front of our place, and Greg convinced him that he needed to get to the hospital, ASAP.

"What does he think he's going to the hospital for?" I asked as I unlocked our front door.

"He thinks his appendix has ruptured."

"That's a good one. What if he gets there and he doesn't have his appendix?"

"Then he won't have to worry about that anymore, will he?"

I plopped down on the couch and tossed my shoes across the room. Greg grabbed a blood bag for each of us, and we started to settle in for a marathon *Gears of War* session. All in all, it had been a pretty good night. We rescued the little girls, I talked to a human woman, we beat the baddy, and we made it home before sunrise. Then my cell phone rang, and the night went right to crap all over again.

Chapter 21

The display on my phone read "Father Mike," so I pushed the button and said, "Hi Dad."

"Jimmy, where are you?" He sounded out of breath, and I was a little worried. Mike's pretty unflappable most days (might be something about having vampires for best friends), so anything that had him running around breathless was bound to be worrisome at best and more likely not-good-at-all.

"I'm home. What's up?" I waved for Greg to turn off the TV. I had a bad feeling that we were going to be heading back out. I got off the couch and walked over to my shoes, cradling the phone between my ear and shoulder.

"Is Greg with you?" Mike asked.

I was really starting to worry now. Whenever Mike wanted to make sure we were together, it meant things were not-good-at-all.

"Yeah, he's here. I'll put you on speaker. Done. What's going on?"

"I'm outside. I'll be down in a minute." He hung up on me.

I stood there for a few seconds looking at my phone, wondering what had him so rattled. Then I put my shoes on and got the place ready for visitors. I motioned for Greg to clear away the empty blood bags. Mike knew what our deal was, but we tried not to flaunt our bloodsucking ways in front of him.

I was in the kitchen dumping out half-empty beer bottles when I heard Mike's feet on the stairs. "Want a drink, Dad?" I called out, trying to keep my voice cheerful. I realized cheerful was wasted as soon as I saw how pale he was.

"Scotch," he ordered. "Make it a double. And you'll want one, too, I believe." He sat on the couch and I brought over our drinks.

"Where's mine?" Greg asked from his armchair.

"Still in the bottle, dork. I might have mad vampire skills, but I still only have two hands."

He stomped over to the kitchen and made himself a stout screwdriver. "You never would have survived in the restaurant business."

"Good thing I didn't survive, then," I retorted. "Now, Mike. You look like crap. What's wrong?"

"You really know how to warm a man's heart, Jimmy. But I'm sure I've seen better days. I don't know if you've been outside recently, but it's terrible out there. I think it might be . . . ," he hesitated for a moment and I saw real fear in his eyes. "I think it might be the end times."

"Whoa!" I stood up and went for more scotch. After a brief debate, I came back to the couch with the whole bottle. "Now let's take this from the beginning. What makes you think that this could be the Apocalypse?"

"Oh, Jimmy, I've seen things in my life that no man should see, and you know this."

"Yeah, I know. We're the ones that showed you most of them," Greg piped up. I shot him a dirty look, and he mumbled, "Sorry," and shut up.

Mike continued. "I've seen plenty of terrible things in my time, but nothing compares to what I've seen tonight. The dead are walking, Jimmy! The newly buried dead have risen from their graves and are walking the town. I don't know what to think, but that these are the times of Revelation!" Mike got a look in his eyes that was part fear, part excitement.

I guess this would be like Christmas, the Super Bowl and WrestleMania all rolled into one for a priest.

"Can you give us a few details? What exactly is going on?" Greg asked.

"Three corpses, all dead less than a month, have risen tonight alone." Mike reached for the bottle, and I passed it over. He touched the neck to the rim of his glass, but his hands were shaking and he rerouted the bottle to his mouth. He glanced at me in apology and turned the bottle up. We'd been friends long enough that I didn't begrudge him drinking from the bottle. It's not like I was worried about germs.

"How many dead people are in your cemetery, Mike?" Greg asked.

"Hundreds, I guess, but what does that matter?"

"I'm wondering why only three have risen, is all."

"Well, they were the most recently deceased. And all of their bodies were intact. One man, Alan Rice, who passed away in the same time period, died in a horrible automobile accident. He has yet to rise."

"Or his body wasn't chosen." Greg mused. "Let me make a couple of phone calls." He grabbed his phone and went into his bedroom. I heard one side of the conversations as he made a couple of calls in quick succession, asking the same questions each time.

"All right, I have a theory," he announced, rejoining us and taking a healthy slug of scotch himself, "and if I'm right, we're going to need more booze. And more ammo. And maybe an extra priest."

Mike and I stared at him until he went on.

"I made a couple of phone calls to a friend at the county morgue and a couple of hospitals. These are not guys who get rattled easily, and they've seen enough of our world to believe in the unbelievable."

I raised my hand. "Excuse me, Professor Doofenstein, is there a point coming anytime in the next week?"

Greg shot me the bird and went on. "You're not the only one missing a bunch of dead people, Mike. The morgue has lost four corpses, the hospitals have lost three, and I'd be willing to bet that at least one more church has seen a rash of breakouts from the graveyard tonight. As far as I can tell, there are nearly a dozen dead people that decided to pull a Thriller on us, and they all made that decision about 11:30 P.M."

"That's when the graves at my churchyard began to cast up their dead. How did you know?" Mike asked.

"Because that's when Jimmy and I set eleven angry souls loose on the greater Charlotte area."

Suddenly a very, very bad light came on for me. "Oh crap. The girls," I said in a very small voice.

"Yep, buddy. Free the girls, free what's in the girls," Greg confirmed.

"What girls?" Mike asked.

We told him all about fighting the little kidnapped girls, and the salt, and banishing them. "But we forgot one important thing," I said. "We forgot to send the souls back to wherever they came from."

"So when they got out of the girls, with no unoccupied bodies around, and no spell to bind them into a body, they went looking for bodies that weren't being used and didn't have salt handy," Greg confirmed.

"They inhabited corpses," Mike said.

He looked a little relieved and a little disappointed all at the same time. I suppose that's how it would be for someone who believed they were about to meet their maker and had reason to look forward to the meeting, then found out that they weren't getting that appointment after all.

"Yep, that's what it looks like." Greg looked altogether too pleased with himself for my taste, but I had to admit it was a brilliant bit of logic.

"Now what?" I asked my occasionally brilliant partner.

"I don't know." He sat down on the other side of Mike on the couch.

"We have to return these bodies to their proper rest," Mike said. "We cannot stand by and allow this evil to be perpetrated."

"Yeah, we got that, but it's the 'how' we're a little fuzzy on," I told him.

"Oh." Mike had another belt of scotch. He hadn't quite moved back to drinking from the glass, and I decided to let the stereotype slide for once.

"Let's look at what we know." I started. "One, there are a total of eleven zombies running around the city. Two, if we don't stop them, at some point between now and tomorrow night, these zombies are going to grab a kid and the demon that raised them is going to finish some humongous ritual that will mean very bad things for everyone in Charlotte. Three, the demon, named Belial, has possessed a woman who looks like a retro advertisement for cookware.

"Now let's take a look at what we don't know. We don't know what they're trying to do in the first place. We don't know if the ritual requires a specific site. We don't know where the zombies are now. We don't know which little girl they're going to kidnap to finish their baker's dozen. And we don't know who the crazy lady with the bun is."

"Now that we've established we don't know anything helpful, where do we go from here?" Greg asked.

"I have no idea."

"I do." We both looked at Mike, who looked a little embarrassed. "I have a friend who practices a religion that the Church . . . um . . . frowns upon. She may be able to be of assistance, at least in the matter of the ceremony and those questions."

"Mike, are you consorting with Wiccans again? You keep this up, and I'm going to put a COEXIST bumper sticker on your station wagon."

"Not consorting. Comparing. She's a local high priestess. She's part of a comparative theology breakfast I attend each month. We've gotten to be fairly friendly over the years."

I looked over at Greg and his jaw was as close to the floor as my own. In all the time we've been friends with Mike, and he certainly shows the years a lot more than we do, we never would have believed that our straightlaced buddy would have breakfast every month with a real live witch. Of course, most of his parishioners would have a harder time believing he was drinking scotch in the basement of a halfway house with two vampires, so I suppose that was only fair.

"Do you think you could call her tonight?" Greg asked. "I know it's getting late, but this is pretty important."

"She once told me that I could call her anytime if I had issues that needed her assistance," Mike assured us.

Greg and I exchanged a glance, and I bit back any comments I might have thought about making regarding Mike's vows of celibacy. He went upstairs to get a signal and make the call, which took only a few minutes. He came down the steps holding his cell phone over his head like he was going to spike a football.

"I assume that means she's on her way?" Greg asked.

"Yes, boys, it does. She'll be here in fifteen minutes. I hope you don't mind meeting her here. After all, the whole 'invite me in' thing could become awkward if we went to her apartment."

"Fair enough, I suppose. Greg, you wanna tidy up a bit before we have another guest?" I asked from my seat on the couch.

"Um, no. Those are your socks, bro. You pick up the toxic waste. I'll give the kitchen a lick and a promise, but the footwear funk factory is all you." He headed off to wipe down the counters and put the blood in the crisper so our culinary restrictions wouldn't be immediately apparent while I got to work straightening up the den.

My idea of straightening up was to pour all the half-drunk beers down the sink and put the bottles in the recycling bin. Not much, but it made the den look better. Then I policed any inappropriate magazines and DVDs that Greg might have left lying around, and threw them all in his bedroom. Mike straightened up the video-game equipment, and actually found a scented candle to put out on the coffee table. After about ten minutes, the place smelled significantly less like a locker room, and Mike had ceased to make comments about us having the hygiene of a pack of feral dogs.

I looked around and nodded to my friends. We were ready to welcome a witch into a vampire lair.

Chapter 22

A knock at the top of the stairs announced the arrival of our guest, followed immediately by a trim pair of legs coming into view on the steps. The legs were, as is par for my course, attached to a woman who looked nothing like my mental picture of an overweight gypsy woman with three teeth and a mole on her nose that had its own zip code. Instead, the woman in our living room was medium height, slim, with straight blonde hair that hung halfway down her back. She was younger than I expected and very pretty in a blonde Sandra Bullock kind of way.

She wore Birkenstocks, but they were the closed-toe type and that was her only concession to my mental image of an earth-mother type. She had on jeans that hugged some pretty nice curves, and a bulky tan sweater that looked like it came straight out of an L.L. Bean catalog. "Hello," she said, her warm voice filling the room with a sense of well-being. "I'm Anna. How are you, Mike? You sounded worried on the phone."

"I was worried, my dear, but I feel much better now that you're here." Mike's accent had slipped, and a little of the old South he grew up in had dropped into his words as he gave the pretty witch a brief, and chaste, hug. Good to know my old friend was celibate, but not blind. He turned to us. "These are my friends, Jimmy and Greg."

He pointed to each of us in turn, and I stepped forward to shake her hand. I was surprised when she pulled back, reaching quickly inside her sweater to drop a pentagram necklace out into view. It began to glow, and I took a quick step back. "Hey now, no need to get all magical in my den, lady," I exclaimed.

"I know you, vampire," she said, and when I looked up at her eyes, they were a cold blue, staring right into my soul. If I had one left. The jury's been out on that one for a while.

"Nope, pretty sure we've never met. But if you want to get together sometime for a quick bite, let me know."

I bared a little fang at her, and heard Greg moving up behind me. His pistol cleared the holster and I knew that he had my back. As long as I kept her attention on me, my partner could keep her covered. "Mike, you want to explain to Mrs. Broomstick here that we're the good guys?"

"It's true, Anna. These boys have been friends of mine since before I entered the seminary. I've known them since we were boys in school together, and they're good lads. They have their problems, sure, but good lads nonetheless."

"Mike," the witch said, keeping her voice level and her eyes locked on me, carefully not looking in my eyes, "This good lad, as you call him, is a vampire."

"And you're a witch," I said. "And by the way, you can look me in the eye, our mojo doesn't work with your necklace in the way. Now, can we get past our little stereotypes and species bias and work together to deal with a body-snatching demon and the zombie infestation?"

"What does my necklace have to do with anything?" the witch asked.

"The boys have some issues with religious symbols, holy ground, that sort of thing," Mike said. "I, for one, believe these issues to be more psychological than pathological." Mike was getting on a roll now, so I went to the kitchen for another beer as he explained one of his pet theories of vampirism to his witch friend.

"The discomfort that they experience around objects of faith is dramatically different from the type of pain that is inflicted by sunlight, and the nausea they experience on holy ground is nothing like the barricade they experience when they attempt to enter a dwelling uninvited. So it's long been my theory that there is no reason that Jimmy and Greg can't touch a cross, for example, or enter a church without any ill effects."

"So why do I feel like barfing every time I go visit you at work?" Greg returned to his spot at the computer.

Mike ignored the interruption and went right on. "No

reason other than their own subconscious fear that they may have lost their souls when they became vampires, that is. And after these past years of working alongside them, helping people at every opportunity, I can assure you, they have every bit as much of their souls as you or I have."

I went back to my spot on the couch and took a seat. Anna followed me with her eyes, then made her way to the armchair and sat facing me. She wasn't paying any attention to Greg.

"Are we good?" I asked as she got settled. "We wouldn't have called you over here, to our home, unless we thought we could trust you, and unless we needed you. Mike was pretty convincing on the first count, and the situation pretty much covers the second."

"What's the situation?" She pulled a MacBook out of her backpack. "Is there Wi-Fi here?"

"Yes," said Greg from where he suddenly stood right behind her chair. I almost fell off the couch laughing as Anna jumped about eight feet straight up. His vamp-speed from his desk to right behind her got the desired reaction.

"The password is TruBlood. Capital *T*, capital *B*," he said as she glared at him. I shot him a look, too, but that was for picking a dorky password.

When I looked back to Anna, the exasperation on my face was from real irritation. "Seriously? You're just going to Wikipedia 'zombies' or something? Any of us could have taken that brilliant first step." I leaned back on the couch, not just to get further away from her glowing necklace, but also because I think she might have caught me checking her out. She's hot. I'm not *dead*. Well, I am dead, but I'm not dead and blind.

"I'm not just going to Wikipedia it. I have a group of friends I can contact online that may have some firsthand knowledge in the area."

"You know people who have their own pet zombies?" I marveled. "Now that's cool."

She sat there for a few minutes typing and muttering to herself and generally looking way hotter than any woman that had been in our tomb in a decade. Or ever, for that matter. After a couple of "hmmms" and the odd "mmmm-mmmm," I got bored and went to the fridge for a snack. Greg immediately plopped down in my seat on the couch and yelled over to me "You keep eating this late at night, you're gonna get fat."

"We can't get fat, dork. You want anything?"

"Yeah, throw me a bag of B-Neg."

I tossed him the bag and hopped up on the bar that overlooked the living room, my own blood bag in hand.

"Either of the humans want anything to drink?" I asked our guests. "We don't have any food, for obvious reasons, but we've got a couple Cokes—"

"Not so much," Greg corrected.

I tried again, "We *had* a couple Cokes, but we've got beer, ginger ale, and a lot of booze. There might even be some orange juice left."

"Again, not so much," my gluttonous partner added.

"Jesus Christ! Do you ever replace what you drink?"

"Heh heh. Nah, I usually count on the marrow to do that for me." We both laughed, because sophomoric vamp humor never goes out of style. It's like a fart joke, only different.

When I realized we were the only ones amused, I sobered. "Anyway, either of you want a drink?"

Anna and Mike replied in the negative. Greg and I drank our blood in silence while Anna worked. Mike looked a little unhappy about us drinking in front of his friend, but she already knew what we were. No point in hiding it. Besides we weren't slurping.

Cold blood is kinda flat tasting, but it's better than room temperature. Obviously it tastes better at body temp, but I didn't want to offend Greg or Mike by going off to hunt. So it was O-positive flavored with plastic and anticoagulants for me. Yippee.

While Anna was hacking away, I turned to Mike. "Hey, Dad? Did you ever find anything more out from the possessed girl?"

"Oh yes," Mike said. "Michelle was her name. What do you want to know?"

"Well, let's start with how she was planning on cursing Tommy Harris and his whole family into oblivion."

"Oh, that." Mike actually sounded amused. "That was actually a mistake."

"What do you mean, a mistake? She didn't mean to curse him?"

"Oh, no. She definitely meant to curse him, she just didn't know how."

"But she did it. I don't get it."

"The little girl had dabbled in some witchcraft, but was by no means a skilled enough spellcaster to actually make a curse stick."

"You're saying she didn't curse Tommy?"

"Not with anything meaningful, no."

"He was never in any danger?"

"Not until you confronted the possessed child with him in tow, no. She was not focused on him any longer, but then you showed up."

"Great. I love my life. This little girl just happened to be the one possessed, and it really has nothing to do with our case at all?"

"Well, it may certainly be the case that her experimentation with magic made her more attractive to outside influence, but that is generally the case."

"This was all a mistake, and we were never needed in the first place?"

"Basically, yes."

"Story of my life." I went for another drink and sat down on the couch to wait for the hacker witch to finish. I leaned over to Mike and spoke in a low voice.

"What do you think, Dad? Is your witchy woman going to be able to tell us how to send zombies back to Hell?"

"Actually, James, we want to be very careful about that. We only want to send the inhabiting souls back to Hell. The bodies we very much would like to return to their resting places," Mike told me.

"Fair enough, Padre. But I'm not digging. I not ruining this manicure digging graves." I was half joking. I've never had a manicure. But I was serious about the no digging part.

"Well," Anna said, finally looking up from her keyboard and stretching her arms over her head. "You'll have to get your hands dirty if you want this to end. My coven is gathering at the fountain in Marshall Park. If we can get all the zombies there by dawn, we can banish the spirits in a sunrise ceremony."

I choked a little at the s-word, but she didn't even slow down.

"Let's go. Get the zombies, incapacitate them, and drop them at the park with my coven. They can bind the creatures long enough for us to exorcise them, for lack of a better term." She looked apologetically at Mike, who gave a little nod. No one wanted him to think we were stepping on his theological turf, but he wasn't terribly well equipped for this sort of thing, dogma-wise.

"That sounds like a plan," I said. "A crappy one that will probably end up with some of your coven having their brains eaten, but it's the best one we have. Any idea how to find these zombies?"

"I'm on that one," Greg piped up. "I've been following police dispatches on my laptop." That really impressed me, since I thought he'd just been messing around on Facebook the whole time. "It seems like the zombies are all converging on one spot. I don't have enough data yet to figure out exactly where that is, but I think I can use the info I do have to get us within a few blocks."

I raised my hand. "Hey, Professor Pugsley, do I even want to try to understand how you're doing that, or should I wait until you give me the signal and then hit something really hard?"

"Let's all play to our strengths. I'll do the computing, Mike will do the driving, Anna's coven will do the banishing and you do the punching."

"Sounds good to me. Give me a minute to gear up and I'll be right with you." I headed over to the coat closet but stopped cold at Mike's voice.

"No guns."

I turned around almost slowly enough to be a parody of myself, and looked at him. "Why not, exactly? I understood the whole no-killing-the-little-girls rule you came up with, because regardless of my membership in the Walking Dead Society, I'm not a *monster*. But Mike, these guys are already dead. It's not like they're going to get upset about it."

"First, you technically are a monster. There are movies to which I can refer you. Secondly, I cannot allow you to defile the dead in my presence. Even though these may be but empty vessels, I am a man of the cloth and cannot allow you to harm the bodies." He crossed his arms and gave me his best priestly gaze.

The priestly gaze works much better on people who didn't steal licorice from the corner drugstore with you when you were seven. "I won't hold your career decisions against you if you don't hold mine against me. And as much as I love you, Mikey, I'm taking the shotgun for the zombies. Get over it."

"Then I'm not driving."

"Fine, we'll take Greg's car." I caught sight of Greg out of the corner of my eye gesturing wildly at me, but I ignored him. Wish I hadn't. As usual, ignoring him turned out to be a bad idea. Father Mike clued me in.

"Greg's car isn't here. You left it at the bowling alley, where it has doubtless been towed to the police impound lot by now."

Crap. I hate it when other people are right. Because it usually means that I'm wrong. And because it happens so much of the time. Now I had to use non-lethal methods to subdue a dozen dead guys, and I had to figure out how to get Greg's car out of hock without ending up arrested. Again. I might have stomped around the room cursing for a minute or two before I said anything intelligible.

"Fine, you win," I said when I ran out of profanity. "We'll do it your way. I'll leave the shotgun, but can I at least take the cricket bat? I bought it special just in case I ever got the chance to whack a zombie with it."

"And you have the audacity to call me a dork," Greg said from behind me.

"Dude, you still wear Underoos. Your geek-fu is so much stronger than mine, it's ridiculous. You are the Mister Miyagi of geek-fu. You are the geek ninja. You are the first person in history to be granted a P.H.Geek from Oxdork University."

"I get it. Here's your bat." He poked me in the stomach with it as he walked to the stairs. He stopped at the bottom of the stairs and gestured grandly to Anna for her to precede him. "To the car, madam?"

"You first, vampire."

Wow, not only was she a witch, but she was a witch with good taste in men. Greg sagged like a kid who's just dropped his favorite GI Joe down the well. He trudged up the stairs, head hanging low. He was so disappointed that his gallantry went unappreciated that he forgot his cape. I grabbed it to cheer him up, wrapped a few surprises in the black fabric, and followed him up the stairs to load the trunk of Mike's car. According to my best guess, we had a pile of zombies to capture and banish, and only about three hours to do it in.

Chapter 23

Greg's math was better than I'd ever willingly give him credit for—we found the first set of zombies about fifteen minutes after we left our place. The nearest church had lost three corpses, all dead less than a month. They were decidedly gross, even with the whole embalming thing. That process is really only designed to make people look good for a few days. After that, it starts to get very George Romero very quickly. At least they had all their parts. I don't know if I could have dealt with pieces falling off all around me.

Anna had briefed me on her plan on the way, so I had a vague idea what she expected from me. My contribution pretty much boiled down to hitting things. I was okay with that. It had been a rough couple of nights, and I didn't mind the idea of some mindless violence. As the car stopped I took stock of the situation. We had three corpses shambling through a strip-mall parking lot on the east side of town. On the one hand, it being the Saturday night before Halloween made passing them off as drunks pretty easy. On the other hand, they had picked a strip mall with a police substation. That would complicate things a little. We'd have to distract the cops.

Mike and Greg were dispatched to the cop shop with a couple boxes of Krispy Kremes to make sure they got the undivided attention of the constabulary. Then Greg put the mental whammy on them while Anna and I took care of the zombie wrangling. The first one was really easy. We put handcuffs on him, tied his feet together, and that was that. No fight, no attempted eating of brains, nothing.

After the first capture, though, Zombie Number Two apparently got a clue we were going to try and block them from their destination, so he fought back. I had one handcuff on the guy, a middle-aged dude who was a little on the heavy side if I'm being particularly kind, when all hell broke loose. His eyes glowed, and he went from shambling, slow '70s-era zombie to *28 Days Later* butt-kicking monster in a split second.

"Look out!" I yelled to Anna as the dead guy threw a haymaker that would have broken my jaw if it had connected. I got out of the way, and backed into the arms of the third zombie, a woman who was probably attractive in life, at least before she got her face mangled by whatever killed her. She grabbed my arms and the guy zombie put one hand on my throat. He drew back with a huge fist, and I dropped out of the way barely in time to keep him from smashing my face flat. He connected squarely with the woman zombie, and she flew across two parking spaces and fetched up against the side of a Toyota minivan.

"Throw me the bat!" I called as I jumped on the hood of a parked car to avoid the guy's next punch. He jumped right up behind me, but I had the bat by then and clocked him a solid shot to the left temple. I was trying to heed Mike's words about not defiling the corpses, but it was gonna be hard if they were this intent on defiling me first. I heard Anna scream and looked over to see her running toward our car with the female zombie in hot pursuit. They were too far away for me to get there before the zombie closed on Anna, so I threw the bat as hard as I could and got a *thunk* on impact that echoed across the parking lot. The female zombie went down hard, and I looked around to find where the guy I decked had fallen.

Except he hadn't fallen. He was standing right behind me, and as I turned he picked me up over his head like a bad pro wrestling show from the '80s and tossed me about twenty feet. I stopped whistling through the air when I went through the windshield of a parked bakery van. The windshield was now one big popped out sheet of rumpled, shattered safety glass, and I now had a close personal relationship with the gearshift. Slowly, I disentangled myself from it and the front seat. I got out of the van and joined Anna back near our car.

"This is not what I had in mind," she said when I got within earshot.

"Me, neither," I gasped. I was pretty sure I had broken a couple of ribs, and while they would heal quickly, they hurt like the devil right then. "But it's not too far from what I expected. Pop the trunk."

"The trunk, why?" She looked at me in confusion.

"Are you one of those women who will never, no matter how dire the circumstances, do anything unless you understand all the reasons behind it? I just want to know, because if I'm going to die because of someone's ridiculous need for exposition, I'll go flippin' stake myself," I snapped. "Now open the trunk because *that's where all the guns are*."

"That's all you needed to say," she huffed. But she did reach into her pocket and get out her key fob to pop the trunk. Greg's cape wasn't the only thing I'd tossed into the trunk while everyone else was getting their seatbelts fastened. Mike and Greg came out of the police station, but stutter-stepped when they saw the chaos in the parking lot.

I got to the back of the car and yelled for Greg. "Get over here, bro, I need backup!" He hustled over and I handed him a twelve-gauge and an aluminum baseball bat. "Knees and elbows. We want the demons to stay locked in the bodies but be unable to move."

"Mike won't be happy."

"Mike doesn't get a vote anymore. That was before we realized the zombies can think and react. We have to disable them and get this done in the next couple of hours or we're going to have a bigger mess on our hands than we've ever dreamed of. Imagine these guys wandering through downtown during rush hour. Now, you with me?" I racked a shell into the chamber because Greg always works better with dramatic sound effects.

He took the bait. He cracked his knuckles and said "Let's do this."

I think somewhere deep in his brain my partner has a folder marked "clichés" that he accesses every time we're in trouble. His ability to quote movies in times of extreme stress is impressive, in a sad kinda way.

We came out from behind the car and followed the two unbound zombies, who had abandoned us when we stopped fighting and returned to their original course. They'd managed to navigate more than halfway across the parking lot and almost to the entrance of a fast-food restaurant. The location was problematic. We were about to shoot a couple of walking corpses right in front of PlayLand, but that really couldn't be helped.

I took out the knees on the woman zombie. Greg couldn't shoot a woman, not even a dead one, so I didn't waste time asking him to take her out. Me, I'll open fire pretty quickly on anything, living or dead, that tries to kill me, hurt me or look at me like it might eat my brain. After the knees, I switched to her arms, and broke both at the elbows with my bat. Greg did the same with the guy zombie, and we quickly bound them hand and foot and tossed them over our shoulders. I hoped the spectators in the window chalked it up to a Halloween party gone wild.

We got back to the car and deposited our cargo, but noticed something was missing—the first zombie. I heard a shouted Bible verse from the back of the strip mall. Our broken zombies wouldn't be going anywhere, so we headed off to save the night. When we got to the back of the mall the missing zombie had knocked Anna out cold and was choking Mike against a loading-dock door. We couldn't shoot without hitting Mike, so I tackled the pile of grave dirt while Greg tended to the wounded.

Every year I swear to sign up for a first-aid class that meets at night so I can play medic while Greg plays linebacker. But, once again, I hadn't kept my resolution so I got the dead guy off Mike and beat the crap out of him with my bat.

The problem with beating on zombies is that they don't feel pain, so you have to do real damage. Going after joints is best, but if they're thrashing around trying to kill you, that's pretty hard. I shattered one elbow, but he got a couple of good shots in before I finally connected with a kneecap. With nothing holding his leg upright, he went down like the corpse he was. I took a couple extra minutes to break his other knee and elbow, then hefted him up across my back and took him to where his buddies were writhing around.

You can't really knock a zombie unconscious, so they were groaning and biting and being generally annoying—which is off-putting in a dead person. I walked over to the local supermarket and got a roll of duct tape, and before too long I'd made three silver-taped and very lumpy zombie Christmas presents. Greg helped Mike and Anna back over to the car, and grinned every second that she allowed him to help her walk. If he got any more excited I was going to put Xanax in his blood bags.

When they arrived we all stood there, panting and bruised—with more than a handful of graveyard dirt and flaky zombie-flesh clinging to our clothes—and took a look at the mess around us. We had managed to break half a dozen cars or so, which I thought was a pretty good record for us. Most of the people parked in the parking lot still had transportation.

Crap. Transportation. I'd stumbled upon a huge hole in our plan. Anna had said she could perform the spell, but even with her whole coven backing her up, it would be a one-time thing. For everything to work we needed all the zombies in one place at one time. Therein lay the rub. We had neglected to address how we were going to carry eleven zombies around until we could banish them. We didn't have a paddy wagon, and we couldn't afford the time to ferry them back and forth to a central collection point after we ran each one to ground.

We needed some way to get these zombies to Marshall Park while simultaneously chasing down the rest of the zombies. And after that fight, we needed all hands on deck to get the job done. None of us had any desire to split up. So I called a cab for our "friends," the zombies.

Even though it was almost Halloween, the deal took a little explaining, a little mojo and a folded hundred-dollar bill, but I got the cabbie to agree to take our three "drunk friends" to the park and deposit them on the sidewalk away from the police station. I told him that me and my fraternity brothers had plenty of partying planned for the night, and if he'd keep his mouth shut and his cell phone on, he could make almost a grand by the time the sun came up. He babbled something about a mother and father and a sick baby, but I didn't really care. I waved half a dozen more pictures of Ben Franklin in his face, and he agreed not to take any fares but my "friends" for the rest of the night. Even after all this time I'm often amazed at what people will believe in the name of cash and a fraternity Halloween party.

Chapter 24

The rest of the zombie encounters went much like the first, with the exception of the car chase. The last dead dude actually made us chase him, in the car, with Greg hanging out the window playing mailbox baseball with his spine. We kept the brain-eater alive, and because Mike had fallen asleep in the backseat long before we got to the last zombie, we didn't get another lecture about defiling the dead.

We tossed Marathon Man in the trunk because I was out of cab fare and I was afraid that even my dreadlocked ganja-befuddled cabbie was starting to think that this was something other than a fraternity stunt.

When we rolled up to join the witches in banishing a passel of angry spirits back to Hell, we had about an hour of night left. Not to mention that a successful banishment would leave us with eleven corpses in Marshall Park, a public space directly across the street from the headquarters of the Charlotte-Mecklenburg Police Department. Of all the places in the greater Charlotte area that I wanted to be when the sun came up, this was nowhere on the list.

We left Mike snoring in the backseat, and I grabbed the dead guy from the trunk. This one was skinny, at least. Some of the zombies we'd bagged that night had been seriously hefty in life, and that made for a slippery, jiggly corpse. If more people toted dead bodies over their shoulders, I'm convinced the obesity epidemic in America would be solved pretty quickly.

There were a dozen witches waiting for us in the dew-covered grass around the fountain in the center of the park. Anna made thirteen. They were arrayed on the concrete steps where countless festival goers and small children have played over the years. I somehow doubted we had the proper city permits for what we were about to do.

Anna explained to us that thirteen was a number of power, like three, seven and nine. I didn't bother to ask more because I really didn't care. I was tired, covered in all kinds of things that flaked off dead people, and had broken and healed ribs twice in one night. Once I even had to heal my arm. That left me hungry, grumpy and smelly—not a good combo for a vampire meeting a dozen witches for the first time. But Anna had carried her weight tonight so I tried. I honestly tried.

"Anna," I aimed to sound cheerful. "Aren't you going to introduce us to your friends?" I made what I hoped was a fang-free and friendly smile all around, but the number of glowing pentacles told me that I wasn't exactly making a harmless impression.

"No, vampire, I am not." Her voice was cold, and I saw Greg's face fall.

I was less surprised to discover we were good enough to hunt zombies with, but not good enough to take home to the coven. Greg falls in love with weather girls, so I wasn't surprised that he'd developed a monster crush on Anna in a few hours. Me, I was just interested in a little nibble, and maybe a little something else. But as hungry as I was, a bite to eat would have been enough.

That wasn't happening. Moving on. "Fair enough, witchy-poo. Where do you want your dead guy so we can finish saving the world?"

She had the good grace to blush a little. "Put him in the circle."

She pointed to where the other ten corpses were arranged carefully in the center of a huge magical circle drawn on the concrete plaza in multicolored chalk, with scribbles and sigils in several languages. I recognized a couple of words of Latin from hanging out with Mike all these years, but just a couple. It wasn't complete. There was about a three-foot opening in the side for me to enter, drop the zombie and exit.

As I got almost to the edge of the circle, something felt out of kilter, and I dropped the corpse on the ground.

"I don't think so," I said. "Your witches can put him in there. I don't want to put his head where his feet should be. I'm all thumbs when it comes to magic, you know." I took a couple of steps away from the circle and turned so that I could see most of the witches and Greg. His face had gone paler than usual at my sudden change of plans.

I caught a glimpse of him taking a position to cover my left, and I concentrated on the witches to my right. Greg and I have been in a lot of tight spots together over the years, and it's nice to have someone you don't have to explain things to when the shit hits the fan. He knew something was up, and went from heartsick to ready to rumble in no time at all.

I didn't actually know if I could be trapped by a circle. Greg and Mike and I have spent a lot of hours researching what made us this way, and we have no idea if we're mystical, extra-dimensional, extra-terrestrial, biological or something even stranger. There's a decent chance the circle wouldn't have bothered me any more than a jail cell made of toilet paper, but I'm never comfortable taking chances that are only decent. I decided to err on the side of caution for a change and not get locked in a magical circle with a dozen zombies on the night before Halloween. Just this once.

Anna spoke from behind me. "Don't you trust us, vampire?"

Her voice had a snide tone to it that I didn't like.

"I don't trust anyone, witchy-poo. It's how I've gone this long without finding splinters in my lungs."

"Well, don't worry, vampire, we won't harm either of you. Tonight."

I didn't like the way she emphasized "tonight," but there wasn't anything I could do about it with sunrise almost over the horizon.

"I'd appreciate it if you didn't harm them, Anna. These boys are under my protection." We all turned at Mike's voice, and I swear my friend looked like he had a glowing halo around him. "I don't think you and yours want to bring down my disappointment, do you?"

When he walked the last few steps to stand next to me I thought the glow might have been nothing more than a street light behind him, but I wasn't sure. It faded as he drew close and whispered, "Thought you'd leave the priest to sleep while all you magical types play in the park, huh? When will you guys ever learn?"

Mike grabbed the zombie by the ankles and started to drag the thing into the circle. The process was made somewhat more difficult by the bandages on his burned hand, but he was strong for a human. The dead guy thrashed around and threatened to scuff the circle, so I grabbed the zombie under its arms and helped Mike carry the animated corpse into the right place in the pattern. I figured the chances of them closing the circle with Mike inside were significantly lower than if I was alone in there, and I knew Greg was keeping a sharp eye out now, so I was willing to help.

Once Mike and I were safely out of the circle, the witches closed it with chalk and mumbling, and then the show started. There was a whole lot of chanting, some smelly stuff thrown into fires at the five points of a pentacle that was scribed within the circle, and a bunch of call-and-response "spellcasting." I was starting to get bored when suddenly the zombies leapt to their feet and rushed at the circle.

They smacked into the magical barrier like it was a wall of glass, and I was exceptionally happy to not be in there with them. They beat on the air, which to them, at least, was very solid, and began to wail. Not the low, guttural kind of moaning that you think of when you think of zombies, but a wail that oscillated like an air-raid siren. It built in volume and pitch until Mike, Greg and I went to our knees with our hands pressed to our heads.

The witches either had earplugs, were deaf, or were protected somehow from the noise, because they kept right on chanting and singing as the keening got louder. Finally, as the zombies literally blew out their voice boxes and their throats exploded with splatters of blood on the air of the magical boundary, silence reigned again. The zombies collapsed to the ground, empty bodies again, and that quiet was the most fantastic thing in the world. I thought for a second that it was all over, that we had sent the souls back where they belonged, but I should have known better.

A new voice came out of the circle, and my blood ran cold as ice.

Chapter 25

"Forgive them Father, for they know not what they do," said the disembodied voice from within the circle. It was a kind voice, a gentle voice, the type of voice that was more soothing than a mother's croon after a nightmare but which also held more strength than a father's sternest lecture. The voice touched a part of me that I thought had died fifteen years ago. Tears rolled down my cheeks at the sound.

I looked over at Mike, and he had the most rapturous look on his face I'd ever seen outside a painting. He stepped towards the circle. He was almost within arm's reach of the boundary when I realized what he was doing. Completely under the spell of the demons in the circle, he was going to break the magical restraints, and all those damned (literally and figuratively) spirits were going to be free again.

I only made it one or two steps before a black blur flew in and knocked Mike sprawling across the grass. The seductive voice turned into a screech of disappointed rage and hurled curses in half a dozen languages at my oldest friend and my partner as they tumbled across the concrete away from the circle. I got a look at a face inside the circle, and if that was what things in Hell looked like, I was glad to be immortal for all intents and purposes.

Greg held Mike down with his considerable bulk and superior strength, and I yelled over at Anna "This would be a great time to wrap this up, lady!"

The witches' chanting grew in volume and intensity, and the light show inside the circle kicked up in earnest. Nearly a dozen angry amorphous, faceless (thankfully) souls whirled and tumbled like psychotic Caspers in a spin cycle, with radiating red, blue and purple lights bouncing around inside the circle like a

Star Wars rerun on fast-forward. The chanting seemed to last forever, but it must have only been a few minutes, because the sky had barely begun to lighten in the east when suddenly the circle fell dark and silent. All thirteen witches slumped to the ground, unconscious. I looked over at Greg and Mike. They had stopped wrestling around and stood staring at the scene on the plaza.

I walked over to Anna and checked her for a pulse. It was strong, and as I felt the blood pulse through the side of her neck, my stomach gave an embarrassing rumble, testament to the long and painful night that had left me hungry. But you don't snack on witches who'd saved the world. Instead, I shook her gently until she began to stir, and I asked quietly, "Is it done?"

She allowed me to help her stand and walk her over to the edge of the circle. She took off her pentacle and passed it over several of the nearest bodies. When it didn't even flicker, she nodded wearily. I helped her over to a bench, and quickly confirmed that all the other witches were still breathing. I avoided the circle, because even if Anna had broken it by leaning over and swinging her necklace over the dead guys, I didn't want to do anything stupid like scrub out a line with my shoe and end up having to fight all these dead guys again.

Turns out the dead guys weren't my immediate problem. Our little light show had attracted the wrong kind of attention. I heard a gentle "*ahem*" sound and turned. Detective Sabrina Law stood on the edge of the concrete plaza, gun in hand and pointed straight at my heart. Obviously, she hadn't taken our disappearance last night in stride.

I hate mornings.

Chapter 26

"Hi Detective." I reached hard for a pleasant, maybe even respectful tone but was really too tired to pull off anything other than half-dead.

"Hi yourself, Black."

"Please, Sabrina, call me Jimmy."

"No thanks, Black. And my first name is Detective." She holstered her gun and reached behind her for a pair of handcuffs.

I snapped at that point. It had been a ridiculous night. I'd gotten handcuffed to a bowling alley chair, had my ass kicked by possessed middle-school girls, chased zombies all over Charlotte, been tossed through a windshield, narrowly avoided being trapped in a magic circle by a coven of witches and I was not about to be handcuffed again, even if it was by the sexiest cop I'd ever seen.

With less concern than usual for the consequences of my actions, I grabbed the cuffs from her, spun her around and snapped them shut on her wrists. With her hands secured behind her back, I tore off a strip of my T-shirt and balled it into a gag.

I turned her back to face me, looked the very angry detective in the face and said, "We are about to get a lot of things straightened out." With that, I tossed her over my shoulder and started toward Mike's car.

"Mike," I hollered back over my shoulder. "Pop the trunk." He and Greg had started moving about the same time I had, and by the time I got to the car with my kicking bundle of detective, they were close enough to open the trunk. I deposited my cargo, making sure not to drop her head on the jack or tire iron, and tucked her long legs into the trunk.

Hard Day's Knight

I leaned down until our faces were inches apart. With fangs on full display, I said, "I'm very sorry you have to ride in the trunk. And I'm very, very sorry about the level of gross going on in said trunk. But you've been a real pain in the butt tonight, and we're going to my place to clear the air. So, I'll be taking this."

I removed her pistol from her side, then grabbed her portable radio. "And this is to make sure you behave on the trip. Oh, and I think I'll take these, too."

Her backup piece was a nice little .38 strapped to one ankle. I also relieved her of her cell phone and her spare handcuff keys. I slammed the trunk shut and got in the passenger seat. It was nice of Greg to read my mood well enough not to make me call shotgun. He got in the backseat and sat there, eyes wide. I told him tackling Mike was a nice save and then stared ahead.

"Let's go home, Mike."

"With her?" he asked.

"Yep. And we should probably not be too concerned about the speed limit or stop lights. The sun's coming up fast, and I'd rather not be a sausage biscuit by the time we get home."

Mike drove like a bat out of hell. He parked his car in back of the cottage, where it would be out of view from the road, and I carried our guest. Then Greg and I hauled ass downstairs before we started to smolder.

"Now here's the deal," I told the detective when I'd dumped her on the couch. "I'm going to take the gag out. Any screaming and I gag you again. We've been through a lot together tonight, and you should know by now that I'm not going to kill you. I'm going to take the handcuffs off, but you can't have any of your guns back until I decide you're not going to do anything irritating like shoot me. Ditto your portable and cell phone. And no one will be tracking you by the GPS in those toys, because I took the battery out of both of them. *Capiche?*"

She nodded and sat there glaring at me, not saying a word even after I took the gag out. I reached around behind her and unfastened the cuffs, and that's when she made her move. She slammed her forehead into my nose hard enough to blur my vision, and shouldered me to the floor as she got off the couch and tried to bolt for the stairs. I grabbed one ankle and pulled her to the floor, and she spun around and kicked me in the side of the head for my troubles. I let go of her leg and lay there for a second as she scrambled to her feet and got into a fighting stance. I thought she was trying to get away, but she just gave herself enough room to maneuver and turned back to kick my ass.

"I don't know who the hell you think you are, but you have messed with the wrong woman, assholes," she said, keeping an eye on both Greg and I.

Greg held up his hands and said, "I'm not the one doing the messing, Detective. That's all my partner's idea."

I'd regained my feet by this point and mimicked Greg's hands-up pose. "We really don't need to do this, Detective. I'm not going to hurt you, and I'm pretty sure you can't hurt either of us."

"Wanna bet?" she growled.

I realized in that moment that there is nothing sexier than a woman who can kick your ass. I shook my head, pushing inappropriate thoughts and images to the rear for the moment, and vamped out on her. I put on a burst of speed and picked up the cuffs from the floor behind her, snapped them back onto her wrists and threw her across the room onto the sofa before she'd even seen me move.

She flopped into a sitting position on the couch and stared at me, eyes a little wild. "How did you do that?"

I crossed the room in less time than it took her to blink and said from the arm of the couch beside her "I have a few talents. Now would you like me to explain them to you?"

She nodded silently.

"Are you sure? We can go a couple more rounds if you'd like, but if our little sparring match goes any further, I'm afraid it will get hard on the furniture. Not to mention you." I hate intimidating women, especially pretty ones, but it had been a *long* night.

"I think I'm good," she said.

"Great. I'm going to let you go now. If you attack me again,

I'm going to knock the ever-loving crap out of you and hang you by your ankles from the rafters. Do you understand me?"

She nodded, a bit wary, and I reached behind her back to uncuff her again. This time we made it through without any headbutting or other unpleasantness, so I gave her back her handcuffs and keys.

"What are you?" she asked after a minute.

"Do you really want to get to the tough questions this quickly?" I asked. "How about a beer first? Or something stronger? We have a full bar."

"Of course you do. Beer is good. Light if you have it."

"Greg, a light beer for the lady. And a bourbon for me, if you don't mind."

He fixed the drinks while I kept an eye on our guest. When he delivered the drinks, he plopped down in the room's one armchair. I got off the arm of the sofa and sat beside Detective Law, who slid as far down the couch as she could and still be sitting. Mike came into the room from where he'd been hiding in the safety of the stairs, grabbed a kitchen chair and pulled it over.

When we were all settled in, I looked over at Detective Law and laid it out for her. "We're going to take a huge chance with everything we're telling you tonight. Usually, whenever we get into a jam that we can't talk our way out of immediately, we mojo the person into forgetting they ever met us. But for some reason we can't mojo you. We're going to tell you the whole story, with no BS. And when we're done, we'll see how you react. If things go the way I think they will, then we all get to figure out what next to do about all this."

"All what? You mean the kidnapped girls and the pile of dead people in Marshall Park?"

"Yeah, that's the beginning of it. There's a lot more crap going on here, but there are some things you need to understand before we figure out what we're doing next."

I finished my drink in one pull and turned back to Detective Law. "We're vampires." I waited, but there was no reaction. "Well?"

"Well, what?"

"Well, don't you have anything to say to that?"

"Look, Jim, I've been a detective for the last ten years. This might surprise you, but you're not the first person I've come across that thinks he's a vampire. I figured that out a while ago. The black clothes, the fake fangs, the nighttime-only business hours. Obviously you're part of some type of vampire cult or something."

I sighed and tried again. "You're missing the point. We're not pretend vampires, we're the real deal. We drink blood, we have fangs, we live underground in a cemetery, for crying out loud."

"Sure, and I bet if I look in your crisper I'll find bags of blood from some orderly you bribed at a hospital, right? And you're fast, but you're no Superman. I live in the real world, pal. I deal with real monsters every day. Don't drag me down here and give me some bullshit about things that go bump in the night. I . . ."

Her voice trailed off to nothing as I pulled her pistol out of my jacket pocket, ejected the magazine, and bent the barrel of her service weapon ninety degrees from normal.

"You wanted Superman?" I asked from my new spot across the room. "Was that strong enough for you?" I was suddenly sitting beside her on the couch again. "And how about fast? Will that do for fast?"

I dropped my fangs into place and leaned in very close to her face. "You're welcome to check and see exactly how real these are if you like, Detective. I could certainly use a snack."

She shook her head, her mouth opening and closing like a flounder on the deck of a fishing boat, so I leaned back to a more acceptable distance, retracting my fangs as I went. "We keep the fangs tucked away until we need them. They make it hard to talk, and they tend to cut our lips if we leave them out all the time."

Mike piped up. "Not to mention the name of the game is for them to blend in."

"We blend as best we can, and, yes, we do indeed bribe a guy at the hospital for our blood supply, but if pressed we can certainly take our meals on the hoof, as it were. Greg pretty much never eats take-out, but every so often I feel the need for a nibble. It reminds me exactly where I stand on the food pyramid—at the absolute top. Now do you believe me?"

She looked from me to Mike and back to me again. She shook herself slightly and refocused on Mike. "But I thought you were a priest? Are you some kind of vampire priest?"

Mike laughed and leaned back in his chair. "I am a priest. A *human* priest. I'm still very much alive, thank you. Jimmy and Greg and I grew up together, and we've been friends for far too long to let a little thing like turning into the living dead get in the way. I trust these boys with my life, and they trust me with their secret. "

She relaxed a little, probably relieved to know that we have a friend that we haven't eaten. "You're really vampires? You and the other one?"

"Yep, Greg. My best friend since junior high and now my undead business partner." I pointed to him and he sketched a rough half bow from where he sat.

"And you really drink blood?"

"Yep."

"And you really can't go out in the sunlight?"

"Poof!" I confirmed.

"Holy symbols?"

"Bad juju for us."

"Stakes?"

"Make us dead as doornails."

"Decapitation?"

"Ruins our night forever."

"Garlic?"

"Total myth. I love Italians."

Law opened and closed her mouth as she realized the distinction I'd just made. I could tell she thought it was funny. Point for me. After a second's pause, she asked, "Running water?"

"I shower every day, so running water is not an issue."

"Silver?"

"Hurts, but doesn't kill. I've never been shot with a silver bullet, and it's not an experiment that I'd care to try."

"How?"

"How what?" I played for time. I figured we'd get to this question eventually. I wasn't really crazy about the answer, but it was going to come out, and I had promised full disclosure.

"How did you two become vampires?"

"That's a long story."

"Well, I have all day. Because I'm not leaving until I'm satisfied you're not as evil as all the stories make you out to be, and I don't think you're going anywhere until sundown."

"All right, but I'm gonna need another drink." I went to get more liquor, and a fresh beer for the lady, and settled in to tell her our story.

Chapter 27

"We were those kids in the corner of the lunchroom, invisible unless you needed someone to pick on. Mike, Greg and I were a modern-day Three Musketeers, tied together by the absence of athletic ability and a remarkable lack of success with women. We made it through high school with slightly more than the normal burdens of angst, self-loathing and wedgies, and off we went to college. Greg and I went to Clemson together. Mike went off to seminary, and we didn't see him again until a whole lot of things had changed."

I looked over at Mike, and he gave me a slight nod. I'd erased some history, especially a big fight the three of us had right before high-school graduation. I'd said some pretty unkind things, including that I never wanted to see him again for the rest of my life. I didn't. I'm not sure that he's ever forgiven me for that. I haven't.

"Greg got a degree in computer engineering, and I managed to flunk, cut, drop and incomplete my way to a BA in English with a minor in psychology." I'd had no idea what I wanted to do except drink beer and play video games, but there's not a degree path in that, so I thought English would be the next best thing.

"One night a few weeks after graduation I met a girl in a bar. Unlike most girls I'd met in college, this one seemed interested. Thanks to my youthful stupidity and tequila, I believed a girl who was *Playboy* hot actually wanted to come back to our apartment with me. Of course, things probably would have worked out very differently if I had looked a gift horse in her mouth, but that would have ruined the story, wouldn't it?"

"I brought her back to the apartment I was sharing with Greg, and we got involved. Then we got very involved. And right as I was about to reach the peak of my involvement—"

"I get it" Detective Law interrupted with a slightly pained expression on her face.

"Sorry. Anyway, just at that special moment, she bit me. And I'm not talking a love nip. I'm talking a fangs-out, attack the carotid, drain you dry kinda bite. So she drained me, in more ways than one, and left me there, on my couch."

"That was cold," Law said.

"Yeah. Stone cold. She left me there, dead and naked from the waist down on my couch, which was how Greg found me a few hours later. And don't think that hasn't made for a few awkward moments in the last fifteen years."

"He found you . . . dead? Alive? Were you a vampire then?"

"I was, and I was *hungry*. Greg got home a couple of hours after she'd killed me, and found my dead, naked body on the couch in front of the television. He tells me that he freaked out a little, checked me for a pulse, and then went to look for the cordless phone to call the police. But the damage was done. When he touched my neck, something inside me snapped awake. I could feel his pulse through his fingertips, and I could almost hear his blood calling to me. I sat up, conscious but not really in control of myself, and when I saw him on the phone, I snuck up behind him and drained him dry in the middle of the efficiency kitchen in our off-campus apartment."

That was a vast oversimplification of things, but she didn't need to know how sweet the blood tasted right from the spring, how amazing and hot and rich it felt as it went down my throat, taking my dead flesh and pouring life into it. It felt like I was forcing his blood down into my desiccated veins, and with every beat of his heart I could feel myself getting stronger, more alive than I had ever been. Everything around me had new color, every sound was crisper, every smell sharper, and the taste was like the most incredible wine and steak and chocolate all rolled into one set of overwhelming sensations.

And as I felt the life drain out of my best friend I didn't care at all about what I was taking away from him, so focused was I on what I was getting out of the exchange. I could hear his heartbeat slowing in my ears, could feel the pulse in his veins getting weaker and weaker with every minute I stayed latched onto him like a pit bull with a T-bone. And I didn't care. I didn't care that I was killing my best friend. I didn't care that I was drinking the life right from his throat like a comic-book monster. All I cared about was how amazing it felt.

"By the time I drank my fill, Greg was dead. I drained him completely, and kept drinking until there wasn't a spare drop lurking in his veins. I really freaked out then, and the only reason I lived through the morning was because I felt too awful about what I'd done to leave Greg's body behind. If I'd run out looking for more food I would have burnt to cinders before I found breakfast."

"I spent the next few hours alternating between freaking out over being a vampire and freaking out over killing my best friend. Every once in a while I'd freak out over how I was going to tell Greg's mom. After a few hours of that, I collapsed on the couch and fell asleep. The combination of dying and coming back to life really took it out of me, I guess. When I woke up it was the next night, and Greg was awake, facedown in the fridge with his head in a bucket of fried chicken."

"Kiss my ass. I was *hungry*," Greg said from his chair. He'd sat through the whole story of his death without saying a word. I knew it still bothered him, but didn't want to try to work group therapy into our confession with the pretty cop-lady.

"I don't remember this asshole killing me, I just remember waking up and being hungrier than I'd ever been before. So I stuck my face in some leftovers and went to town. That turned out to be a really bad choice, since I was no longer able to process solid food.

"Fortunately, I was in the kitchen, so I was able to make it to the sink before the entire contents of my stomach came up in a spectacular mess. That left me hungrier than ever, and I could smell something coming from the living room, and it smelled good. I went in there to see what was for dinner, and the only thing there was Jimmy."

I picked up the thread here. "By now I'd guessed a little

about what was going on, and I had opened a vein in my wrist for Greg. He proved my theory right, and latched on like his life depended on it. Greg drank from my arm, and when I started to feel my strength lessen a bit, I pulled him off me. It wasn't easy, but I got him off my arm. A few seconds later, he calmed down, and I explained to him what I thought had happened."

Greg took over again while I went for another round of drinks. "As far as we can tell, the trait of vampirism is only passed on when the donor is drained completely. If the heart doesn't stop, the donor does not become a vampire."

"What about animal blood," she asked. "Does it work?"

"Nope," I answered. "Apparently there are nutrients in human blood that we don't get from animals. Now, we haven't tried gorillas, or animals that genetically close to humans, but after a few experiments with rabbits and cats we gave up on animals. And I wasn't much of a pet guy when I was alive, so being dead has done nothing to increase my desire for a fluffy puppy."

"And for myself," Greg said, "I have all I can handle trying to domesticate Jimmy, so I've never bothered to try to have a pet. But back to the story. In short, I fed from Jimmy, and then we went out to top off the tank, as it were. We didn't drain those first donors completely, more out of satiation than out of any moral compunction against killing them. We just got full. Once we were thinking clearly, we realized that killing a bunch of random people would be a good way to get caught, and that would probably lead to unpleasant things happening in government laboratories, so we went for a more low-profile route."

There was a lot more to those first few nights than Greg was sharing, but even Mike didn't know much about what we did when we first turned, and I was content to keep all that between the two of us. Let's just say we became much more discreet in our later years.

Detective Law finished off her beer and leaned back in her chair. It was a long moment before anyone spoke, and when she did, the rest of us leaned in to hear what she had to say. "So you're vampires. And you're detectives. And you try to help people. But you still drink blood."

"Yeah," I said. "That pretty much covers it, using broad brush strokes."

"Fair enough. And I suppose you can call me Sabrina. After all, I know more about you than I ever really wanted to know, so I suppose we should be on a first-name basis."

"Now you know our story. And while I enjoy your company more than I have that of any living woman in nearly twenty years, I'm tired. And somewhere out there is a crazy bun-headed demon lady with a plan to do something really nasty to the world. And tomorrow night is Halloween, when crazy people tend to do nasty things. I'm going to get some rest, so that when it comes time to punch, stab or shoot something, I'm ready."

Greg yawned and mumbled his agreement, and headed off to his room.

Mike stood and gathered his things. "As much as I like you boys, your housekeeping leaves much to be desired. I think I shall retire to my parish house and get a little shut-eye myself."

"What about me?" Sabrina asked.

"What about you?" I asked right back. "We're getting some sleep. I suggest you do the same. Go home, Sabrina. Get a nap, get some fresh clothes, and meet us back here at sundown. You know we won't be going anywhere until nightfall, so you don't have to worry about us leaving you out."

"Fine, but this is my case. If you try to shut me out of this, I'll show back up here at noon one day and give you a stake dinner you'll never forget. Deal?" She stood and stuck out her hand. I stood up, too, because that's how I was raised.

I took her hand and shook. Her skin was so warm against mine, so alive that for just a minute I really, really missed being alive. "Deal." I stood there and watched her walk up the steps and into the sunlight, and felt the darkness settle into my chest as she closed the door behind her.

I stayed for a minute staring at where she'd been, until Greg came over, gave me an awkward pat on my shoulder, and said,

"She's so out of your league it's not even funny. Now go to bed." And I did, feeling more alone than I had in years.

I was gonna have to bite somebody that night. To make me feel better, if nothing else.

Chapter 28

I slept for a long time, almost to dusk, and when I woke up, I felt like I'd barely gotten any rest at all thanks to dreams of Sabrina. Great. I love taking on a huge fight after a crappy day's rest and while I'm carrying around pent-up sexual tension. I should have bitten her and gotten it out of the way. I walked into the living room, and found Greg still sitting at his computer. It wasn't that unusual for me to come out and find him facedown on the keyboard, but this time he was still awake.

"I think I know what the plan is for tonight," he offered as I rummaged in the crisper for breakfast. He'd obviously slept very little, if at all.

"Yeah, dude. We had that covered before we went to bed. We wait here for the hot cop chick, then we find the ugly demon-possessed chick, kick her butt back to Hell, and then hopefully I get to second base with the hot cop chick." I jumped over the back of the sofa and landed with my feet on the coffee table. Sometimes the enhanced agility that came with being undead was handy.

"Don't you think the hot cop chick might have something to say about that?" Sabrina's voice came from the stairs, and not for the first time I wondered why mental telepathy didn't come with all the other fringe vamp benefits.

"Nah," I replied, trying to salvage some measure of my self-respect. "Once we save the world there's no way she'll be able to resist my charms. Breakfast?" I held the blood bag out to her.

"No thanks, I ate on the way over. And I have faith in my ability to resist your charms. And in the necklace my daddy gave me at my first communion." With that, she fished a delicate cross out of her shirt and dangled it from her fingertips.

"That's mean." I leaned back on the sofa and finished my breakfast. "G, what was that about a plan?"

"I think I know what Bun-Head is up to," he said, his tone still flat. I was gonna have to spike his next meal with Red Bull or he'd be useless in the fight to come. Then what he said registered and I was over his shoulder in a matter of seconds.

"Seriously? You've figured out her plan? How?"

"The magic of the interwebs. When you went to bed, I couldn't sleep, and we had no idea what Bun-Head's next step was going to be. So I went back to her first steps to see if I could come up with some other nexus between the abductions. And after a couple of false starts, I came up with the answer—school staff."

"Huh?" I asked. "That doesn't make any sense, bro. Teachers only teach at one school. How could someone work at a dozen different schools?"

"She doesn't. At least not permanently. Our bad guy, or in this case, girl, is a substitute teacher. When I ran the lists of substitute teachers in the system against the abductions, one name popped out as being at each school right around the date of the abductions. Janet Randell. She's been a sub for two years now since losing her job as a teacher's aide to budget cuts. She was at every single school the day of or the day before a kid went missing. So I did a little work to find out where she is today."

"And where is she?" Sabrina asked.

"That's where things got a little tricky. She wasn't working anywhere in the district today. But I knew she would have to be somewhere, at a decent-sized school, since she needed a dozen victims in short order. I widened my search, and found her at Holy Trinity." He leaned back in his chair, arms crossed over his round belly.

"How could she guarantee that she'd be teaching today, much less be at a large enough school to find a dozen likely victims?" Sabrina asked.

I was glad she did the asking. Not only did it save me the trouble, but Greg wouldn't razz *her* for not figuring everything out ahead of time.

"She created a vacancy. The home-ec teacher at Holy Trinity was found dead in her apartment last night. Our Janet killed the teacher and set herself up as the sub on call so she could be close to her victims."

"Nicely done, partner." Had to give him his props. "That gives us a location to start with."

"And end with," he said.

When Sabrina looked a question at us, I said, "Holy Trinity is a pretty tightly wound place, the kind of school that teaches Book Burning 101 and pickets rock concerts. Every Halloween they hold a religious fall carnival to combat the Satanic holiday's influence on our children."

"Lucky for us," Greg added, none too happy, "they'll be hosting this carnival tonight at the school gym."

"Crap." I actually paced a small circle as my brain worked it all out. "There will be hundreds of kids and parents there. If the final summoning needs a sacrificial component, then that would be the perfect place to do it."

I looked up. Both of them were staring at me, slack-jawed. "What? Just because I didn't do the research I can't come up with something more profound than 'Hulk Smash?'"

"Yeah," Greg said. "True enough. We concentrate on the fall carnival, because that's where she'll most likely be. And we go over there, ruin her plans, and save the world from something we don't really understand."

"What if we're wrong?" Sabrina looked from Greg to me, and back again. "I think it sounds like a good plan. And all the logic works. It makes perfect sense. But life isn't always logical and doesn't always make any sense. What if we're wrong? What happens then?"

"Then we all die," a deep voice said quietly before I could answer.

Stunned, we all turned to the stairs. *Phil.* But not my Phil, the one I'd come to know and despise. This was Zepheril, the fallen angel, accompanied by Lilith, the first wife of Adam. Phil had his wings on display, and Lilith had on an outfit that put almost all of her on display.

They looked like extras at a fetish party, only better armed. Phil had black leather pants and a sword belt with a sword on it. Lilith wore thigh-high boots with come-hither heels, a black leather miniskirt and a leather jacket unzipped enough for me to see that the only other thing she had on besides a bra was a shoulder holster. The first guy to build a combo bra/shoulder rig that's comfortable will make a mint.

I blurted, "What the hell are you two doing here?"

Lilith gave me a little smile and came over to me, oozing sex with every step. As she approached, the room suddenly felt really warm, and my jeans suddenly felt very tight. Out of the corner of my eye I could see Greg wiping a bead of sweat off his forehead. Sabrina just looked grumpy.

"Why, we're here to help, little vampire. If tonight goes poorly for you, it could go very, very poorly for us." She spoke into my ears in a low voice, almost a purr, and I remembered the feeling of her blood pulsing through my veins.

Pulling back took almost everything I had. I poured all my reserve strength into looking, very carefully, into her eyes, which seemed about the only safe place I could look. "What do you mean, go poorly for you?"

She chuckled and pulled back from me, giving Sabrina a glance as she crossed back towards the door. "You have no idea what awaits you in the afterlife, little vampire, if you even have one. Zepheril and I, however, know exactly what is waiting for us. And that's why we have no interest in bringing about the end of our lives anytime soon. Because what we have in store is unpleasant beyond your wildest dreams."

Zepheril put a hand on her arm and spoke when she paused. "All that is important is that our interests align with yours for the moment. It is time to go."

"Oh, hell no!" Sabrina said from where she had stationed herself with her back to a wall and a clear line of sight to everyone in the room. "I am not going anywhere with Tinkerboy and his partner, Slinky the Super-Slut. I agreed to work with you two because there's no other way to get this case solved, and I still only halfway believe in vampires. But I am not going into a firefight with a couple of . . . of . . . whatever you are at my side!"

Phil crossed to her quicker than anything I'd ever seen. I mean, he made me look positively glacial. He literally appeared at her side and whispered something in her ear. She pulled back, tears in her eyes, and slapped at him. He caught her wrist and looked deep into her eyes. A long moment passed with them staring at each other. I strained to hear what was said, but it was too low even for my vamp hearing. I looked to Greg and pointed at my ear, but he shook his head. Nothing there, either. After a few more interminable moments, Sabrina sagged a little and Phil let go of her hand.

"Now can we go?" he asked quietly, and for a second Phil didn't look like the self-righteous jerk I'd come to know and half despise. He looked like he must have before he fell, kind, peaceful, caring. I didn't like it, so I was happy when his normal sneer came back.

"Are you okay?" I asked Sabrina.

"No. But let's go. We need to finish the job."

Sabrina shouldered her way past Lilith and hurried up the steps ahead of everyone. I wanted to make some crack to Phil about taking a sword to a gunfight. *Desperately*. But after his little encounter with Sabrina, I knew better than to push my luck by making a joke. Instead, Greg and I followed, stopping at the closet to gear up. I wasn't sure how much good my guns would do in this mess, but it made me feel better to strap them on regardless.

And to make things even more festive, Mike was leaning on the fender of his Lincoln Town Car when we got upstairs. I'd harbored a sliver of hope that we could get rolling before he got here, but I should have known better.

"Going somewhere?" he asked. "I knew you wouldn't be able to come out before nightfall, so I did a little research on our demon, and thought you might like to know exactly what it is that we'll be facing tonight."

"Not we, buddy. You're staying home."

"Not likely, old friend."

"This is not a matter for discussion."

"Then let's not discuss it. I'm going with you, and when you hear what I have to say, you'll agree that you need all the help you can get." Then his mouth dropped open at the sight of Zepheril coming up the stairs.

I had to admit, he made an impressive picture, what with the wings, the sword, the six-pack abs. Mike flapped his mouth open and closed a couple of times then said, "Well maybe you do have enough backup after all."

Zepheril stepped over to the stunned priest and put a hand on his shoulder. "No party is so strong that it cannot be aided by a true man of faith. We would be honored to have you accompany us."

I try not to argue with angels as a rule, even (or maybe especially) fallen ones, so I hopped up on the trunk of Mike's car and asked, "What did you find out?"

He took a deep breath, shook his head, took another deep breath, and finally started to speak. "You told me that the demon identified herself as Belial. Having certain resources at my disposal that most people do not, I went back to the church and did a little research. Belial is one of the most powerful of the second-tier demons. She is the child of Baal, one of Lucifer's Archdukes. Baal is the ruler of the seventh circle of Hell, which houses the most violent of sinners. All the murderers, rapists, suicides and blasphemers end up in the seventh circle, and Baal has complete dominion over them. That wasn't a dominion that came to him by default. He's earned his place. He is simply the meanest, nastiest demon in all of Hell and there isn't anyone that can challenge him. Not and win."

Phil and Lilith's interest was suddenly clear to me. "And Belial is daddy's little girl?"

"Exactly." Mike reached into his pocket and pulled out a rosary, holding it like a talisman. "Legend has it that she is the offspring of Baal and the Whore of Babylon."

Mike went on. "If Belial brings Baal to Earth, then he would have complete dominion over this realm, just like he does over the seventh circle. Baal is a force of nature, a creature so powerful that even the angels fear his power. If the ritual completes and the sun rises on Baal in this world, then the entire world will belong to him. He will, in effect, create a Hell on Earth."

The wise men of the world are right. Ignorance really is bliss.

Chapter 29

I stood up and started pacing. "All the more reason why you're staying here. I will not be responsible for taking you into a gunfight with a demon."

"Bite me. And I mean that figuratively, of course," Mike replied.

"Seriously, Mike. We can't take you with us. It's too dangerous. I don't know what I'd do if anything happened to you," Greg added.

"Nothing's going to happen to me. And regardless, I'm a grown man. I get to make all kinds of bad decisions for myself. I can drink a little too much, eat too much red meat, and consort with undead creatures if I choose. And really, is this going to be significantly more dangerous than having my two best friends be vampires?"

"Yes. Because we've never wanted to kill you. Strangle you a little, but never really kill you. If what you're saying is true, this demoness is far more dangerous than anything we've ever faced outside of a video game." Greg managed to stay calm, which was more than I could say for myself.

"How do you plan on handling her if she's so . . ." Mike's voice trailed off as he took a good long look at Lilith. "Oh. Now you can consort with demons, but I'm not good enough to come with you?" His voice was cold, and the look he gave me was heavy with disappointment, and something else I couldn't quite figure out. Maybe fear?

"I'm not consorting with them, Mike, I'm using them. They're tools, and like a cheap hammer, they're tools that I don't care about. You, I care about. I don't give a rat's ass if Lilith doesn't make it out of this alive, assuming she's technically alive now, but you're one of my best friends. And I only have two friends, so I can't afford to lose any of you. Please, I'm begging you, don't give me any grief, just stay home."

"No. I'm going with you, and I'm old enough to be stubborn about it. Who's riding with the holy man?" He raised his voice on the last so that everyone else could hear him.

Greg yelled "Shotgun!" and hopped in the passenger seat. I shook my head in defeat and went to get in Sabrina's car. Phil and Lilith started toward Mike's car, but when they saw the look on Mike's face, the fallen angel and his servant changed direction and wordlessly got in the backseat of Sabrina's much smaller sedan. Phil's wings vanished, and I didn't even bother to ask where they went.

"Don't you two have a car?" I asked.

"No," Lilith answered simply.

"Then how did you get here?" I asked. There was silence in the car for a long moment, then I thought about it for a second and got the mental image of Phil carrying Lilith as he flew along Independence Boulevard during rush hour. "I bet that was something for the commuters to see, huh?"

We rode in silence across town to the school and pulled into the far end of the parking lot. Sabrina popped the trunk and pulled out a pair of pistol-grip twelve-gauge shotguns. She handed one to me and started loading oddly colored shells into hers.

"What are those?"

"Bean-bag rounds. Non-lethal, but they'll take almost anyone out of the fight. Plenty here for you, too. Let's try not to kill any civilians if we can help it."

"I don't mind that in concept, but in practice, the civilians are likely to be the only things we *can* kill. I've got a bad feeling about whatever is in there waiting for us."

"Me too." She looked nervous, and I reached out to touch her arm.

"Hey. It'll be fine. We're the good guys." I tried to manage a smile filled with bravado and cocky charm, but I think I looked more like I was about to puke.

I felt more like I was going to puke, for sure. And as our

motley crew made our way across the parking lot, I felt worse. The closer we got to the school, the worse I felt. It wasn't nerves, or a bad bag of blood. *Something* was messing with me. I looked around at the rest of the gang and saw that Greg was decidedly green as well. Even Phil and Lilith looked like breakfast wasn't settling well in their stomachs. We were about twenty yards from the entrance to the school gym, when I saw the huge banner across the front of the building proclaiming, "Fall Carnival for Christ!—No HELL-oween here!"

"Ahhh, crap," I said. "We've got a problem." I waved everybody together. Sometime between leaving our place and getting to the school, Phil and Lilith had magicked their outfits into something more early 2000s yuppie than late '80s goth porn. I didn't ask how they managed that trick. I really didn't care right now.

"What's the problem?" Mike asked. "I mean, I certainly don't agree with their odd bias against Halloween, but the rest of our plan seems to be solid."

"Except for one thing—location," I said. I looked around at my queasy partner, and the near-dead-looking Lilith and Phil. Mike and Sabrina looked fine, but that also made perfect sense. "The whole school seems to be consecrated—

holy ground."

"Oh crap," said Greg. I watched the realization creep across the faces of the rest of our group as well.

"What do we do?" Sabrina asked. "How do we get in there and get the job done without our heavy hitters?"

"We just do it, my dear," Mike answered. He reached over and took my shotgun, racked a shell into the chamber and pulled out his crucifix. "You and I go in there and drag our little demoness out into the parking lot where our compatriots can send her back to Hell. And don't forget, I brought a little backup myself. And I daresay he's the heaviest hitter of all."

"I can personally vouch for that." Phil handed Sabrina his pistol. "Silver rounds. I don't know what effect they'll have, but it can't hurt."

He passed a few extra magazines around to the rest of us

from his apparently bottomless coat pocket. I didn't question the supply, because I didn't care how he got them or where they came from as long as the rounds gave us an edge in the fight to come.

"Thanks." Sabrina took the gun from Phil, tucked it into the back waistband of her pants and nodded to Mike. "Let's go."

"As they say in the movies, my friends, we'll be back." My old friend looked a dozen years younger as he shouldered the shotgun and headed off to fight a demon in a school gymnasium. If I squinted, I could even make myself ignore the bandages he was sporting on one hand and the limp he had picked up fighting zombies all over town last night.

"Do you think they've got a chance?" I asked Greg.

"I can only hope, bro. For all our sakes."

Chapter 30

I wasn't a patient man. I'm a less patient vampire. I paced the parking lot, growing crankier than hell with each passing moment and no word or indication of what was going on inside. I looked over at where Greg sat on the tailgate of a nearby pickup.

"How long have they been in there?"

He made a show of checking his watch and said, "About three minutes."

"I hate waiting."

"We can see that." Phil was sitting cross-legged on the roof of a minivan, with Lilith beside him.

I started toward the door of the gym, in earnest this time, knowing that forces were in motion against my making it onto consecrated ground. But I'd never tested myself to my limit of endurance. Maybe if a vampire were determined enough, he could make it.

The place pushed back at me, like I was trying to walk through a hard wind. The closer I got, the harder it seemed to push against me, and the sicker I felt. I had gotten almost to the front door when I heard shots ring out from inside. The boom of a twelve-gauge shotgun is unmistakable, and the sound I heard was two of them firing in the kind of rapid succession that would require a fast reload if the job wasn't done.

After about half a dozen shots, the gunshots stopped, and then it got quiet. Too quiet, as the cliché goes. No screams, no running feet, none of the sounds I would expect from a crowded school carnival whose attendees had to contend with a couple of nutjobs unloading a pair of shotguns. The silence reigned for about half a minute, as I kept pushing at the invisible barrier keeping me out. Then a low *whir* reached my ears.

The sound started slow and low, picking up in pitch and intensity, like a jet engine ramping up for takeoff. The noise built for a few seconds, then an explosion from inside sent blinding light out of every window and blasted me back from the doors.

I had almost enough time to gather myself for another assault when the doors of the gym opened up and a stream of people poured out, running like the hounds of hell were on their heels. Which, for all I knew, was true. A couple hundred people ran out into the night, a few of them getting into their cars and careening off down the street, but most just left their cars and ran for home rather than risk the traffic jam in the parking lot.

Phil, Lilith and Greg had pushed their way to my side, and as the stream slowed to a trickle, a familiar figure lurched into view. Mike bounced down the central steps of the building, holding onto the handrail like a sailor on shore leave. Instinctively I broke toward him, expecting the same intense pushback of consecration this close to the building, but there was only a slight roiling in my gut so I kept moving.

I shouted to the others as I ran, "I can make it. Whatever caused the explosion must have weakened the holy hold on the land."

"Mike, are you okay?"

He had a dazed look on his face, and his eyes were out of focus. I had to repeat myself a couple of times to get his attention. When I got through the crush of people, I saw that my friend's hair had gone completely white, like the good guy in a bad horror movie. "Are you okay?" I repeated, and he seemed to come to himself a little.

"What happened? Where's Sabrina? Did you kill the demon?" Greg peppered Mike with questions faster than he could answer. I waved Greg off and then pulled Mike around to the other side of the car.

"She's an innocent, Jimmy." The words were less than a whisper, and I probably wouldn't have understood what he said without my vamp hearing.

"Who's innocent? The teacher? Nah, man, she's the bad guy, I'm pretty sure. What happened in there?" I couldn't follow

Mike's line of thought, and I wondered if he'd taken a smack to the head.

"No. Sabrina. *She's* an innocent, Jimmy. In the full meaning of the word. That's how she got caught."

My borrowed blood ran cold as what he said started to sink in. "The demon has Sabrina? Because she's a . . ."

I didn't say "virgin." Just because I'd heard of them didn't mean I necessarily believed in them any more than unicorns. Not grown women virgins. Sabrina was a grown woman. And hot. A hot, adult virgin in today's society? I might be the vampire standing in the parking lot fighting a demon with a fallen angel and an immortal feminist, but pegging Sabrina as a virgin was a leap of logic I'd never have made.

"This is unfortunate." Phil has a talent for understatement. Obviously.

"Yes. Belial has her. Her and a dozen children. We haven't got much time, we have to get in there and stop the ritual before—" He collapsed against a nearby car, coughing. There was a little blood as he coughed, and I wondered what kind of beating he'd taken in there.

"Mike, I wish we could." Greg was starting to freak out, and he always talks really fast when he freaks out. "But it's sacred ground. We can't go in and help. You've got to do it. You're the only one that can save her." That last bit was more like 'theonlyonethatcan*saveher.*'

He hadn't quite lapsed into "Help me Obi-Wan Kenobi, you're our only hope," but we were getting close. Mike tried to stand, but collapsed again.

"Well," I said, letting Mike slide down to a sitting position beside the car. "I guess it's time to test a theory."

Chapter 31

"Oh, *hell* no!" bellowed Greg, as Lilith looked at me and said "What theory, little vampire?"

"Dude, it's the only way," I replied. I looked over at Lilith and said, "Come along, sister, I think you're on this ride, too." I walked towards the entrance, with Greg walking backward in front of me, both hands out.

"You can't go in there, man. We've tried it before, and it doesn't end well. Even if you make it, we can't function on holy ground." He finally got both hands on me and stopped my march to the gym.

"Yeah, but we've never figured out why, have we? Mike has always said that it was our subconscious hang-ups making us sick whenever we went near a church, not anything having to do with our vampirism."

"Are you willing to take that chance?" Greg looked me in the face. "Is she worth it?"

"I don't know, and yes, I'm willing. Now either come with me or get out of the way. And Lilith, get your immortal tookus up here. I need a little pick-me-up." She came up beside me and gave me a sultry gaze. "Hold the smolder, appetizer. I just need the blood."

She pouted a little. "You're no fun when you're being all heroic, little vampire."

"Maybe after I save the world, get the girl and ride off into the sunrise we can play a different game. But for right now, give me your arm, please." She stretched out her wrist to me, and I drank. Not a tentative sip like the last time, but a full gulp of immortal blood. I saw the look on Greg's face, and it mirrored the fear in my gut. I didn't want to end up a slave to an eternal succubus for the rest of my potentially very long life, but I had to get in there and rescue Sabrina. I'd gotten her into this mess, and if it took the end of my free will to get her out of it, well so be it.

The power of ages crashed over me like a wave, and I could feel the sensation of it rolling through me. I could almost feel myself getting taller (the last thing I needed) and stronger (the intended result) and even sexier (a new sensation altogether). I drank for a few seconds, and let her go, feeling more alive than I ever had when I was alive. One step toward the gym and I knew the consecration was weakened. It was now or never.

I looked at Greg and said, "You might want to top off the tank, too, old buddy. I think we're gonna need it. Now is not the time to stand on principle."

Then I pushed past him and headed up the stairs into the church gymnasium to fight the demon that had kidnapped my maybe-someday-if-I-get-really-lucky girlfriend. I wasn't certain which was least likely—besting the demon or winning the girl.

Chapter 32

The gym looked like a cross between *Buffy the Vampire Slayer* (the lame movie, not the badass TV show) and Vacation Bible School. There were prom-style decorations from 1993, glittery letters and bunting strung all around the gym, and cheap poster-board signs over booths with slogans like "Bobbing for Salvation," and "Baptismal Dunking Booth." I couldn't decide whether to laugh or cry at the crazy attempt to de-monsterize Halloween, and felt no small irony that a couple of monsters were crashing the party trying to save the children of parents who would most likely lead the pitchfork party if they knew we existed.

My attention quickly locked on to our friendly neighborhood demon summoning taking place right at center court. The bun-headed lady from the forest was standing in the middle of a glowing circle, and there were a dozen little girls playing ring-around-the-psycho. The kids all faced out, and they all had the same glowing eyeball thing going on as the first bunch we rescued. The kids ranged in age from high-school girls down to one kid that looked barely old enough to go to middle school, but that wasn't the worst part.

No, the worst part was Sabrina. She was floating over the center of the circle, a good ten feet in the air over the bun-headed woman, and it looked like a rope of energy was flowing from each of the kids up to where she floated. As we watched, Bun-head twisted her hand in the air, and Sabrina turned in the air until she was looking straight at us. Her hands extended to the sides and her feet crossed at the ankles in a grotesque mockery of a crucifixion, and the look on her face was pure agony. I took one look at her writhing in pain and launched myself at the witch.

I flew a good twenty feet, landed and took another huge leap, crashing right into the invisible wall of the circle. I slid down to the floor like the coyote in one of those old cartoons, and heard the witch laugh maniacally as I lay crumpled on the hardwood floor. I heard several loud cracks like handclaps and looked up to see Greg shooting at Bun-head and screaming something that I couldn't hear through the ringing in my ears and the chirping of those imaginary birdies that were circling my head. The witch kept laughing as the bullets bounced harmlessly to the ground.

"Did you morons really think you could come in here and stop me that easily?" she asked, as she started to glow herself. The energy from the twelve kids was passing through Sabrina and down into Bun Lady, making her eyes glow and her hair unravel.

"Well, I kinda hoped," I said from where I lay on the floor. "Since our frontal assault didn't work, I don't suppose you have a better idea?" The last was to Greg, who had stopped shooting when it became apparent that he was doing no good.

"I got nothing, bro," he replied.

I tried to come up with something, but between the throbbing in my face from crashing into the circle and the nausea in my gut from being on holy ground, it was getting pretty hard to think.

Bun-head began to chant in some arcane language. The lights coming from the little girls glowed brighter, and Sabrina screamed as the flow of power through her became unbearable.

I beat on the barrier and yelled at Greg for help to get her out of there. "Salt!"

He tossed a fistful at the circle, but it bounced off like everything else we threw at it. "No good!" he said. "The circle is complete and only the caster or someone stronger can break it."

I didn't care about the reasons it wasn't working. I didn't care about anything except that the one living person I'd felt any connection to in a couple decades was on the other side of that magic barrier about to be possessed by a serious bad guy while I was stuck on the outside, unable to do anything about it.

Then Sabrina started to spin, and the light flowing through her started to go supernova. The faster she spun, the brighter she glowed, and the louder she screamed. Bun-head chanted in the unfamiliar language as the ground beneath her began to glow in answer to the light pouring down out of Sabrina. The glowing bands of energy started off white, but shifted to red. Then I noticed the kids in the circle starting to change.

There was no way this was going to end well.

Chapter 33

The only word I have for what the kids turned into was *demon*. I don't know if there's a better word, or if there's some type of hierarchy of Hell that I'm offending with my oversimplification, but when I see a four-foot-tall thing with red skin, horns and a spiky tail where a little girl stood a couple of minutes before, *demon* is the word that leaps to mind, and I don't care what the ACLU has to say about racial profiling.

I was still kneeling on the floor when the herd of demons broke loose from the magical circle and charged me and my partner. I was trying to figure out how to beat the demons without hurting the little kids probably still trapped inside, when Greg stepped up beside me and, without hesitation, shot the nearest monster right between the eyes. It flew backward into the circle and lay still. I tried to process that my partner, the vegan vampire who wouldn't even feed off bunnies, hadn't given a rat's ass whether or not a little girl was still inside the demon.

"I have a few issues left over from being tossed naked into the girl's locker room in sixth grade. I've decided to think of this as therapy." He turned faster than anyone but another vampire could follow and dropped another pair of demon girls before they could close on us.

"Dude! That was almost thirty years ago!" I yelled as I kicked a little girl across the gym.

"Some wounds take a long time to heal, man." He plugged another kid, and I started to worry. This was too easy. The demon children were dying just like any human, only redder, with the pointy extremities I'd expected from evil minions.

Apparently I was right, because that's when three of the demons got to me at the same time. I took one by the throat, and fended another off with the other arm, but the third one jumped on my back and bit the side of my neck.

I hate irony.

I bludgeoned the second kid with the first one, and tossed them both to the far side of the room. The kid-thing on my back was really beginning to annoy me. I reached over my shoulder and grabbed a handful of demon hair. It took a couple of tugs, but the little brat finally came loose from my neck, and I pitched her over to join her friends beneath one of the basketball goals.

I drew my Glock and started plugging away at demon children, who apparently weren't bulletproof, just annoying. For every demon that I managed to kill, an unconscious little girl appeared in its place. I didn't understand the transformation, didn't have time to ask anyone who would know, and frankly didn't care all that much. All I knew was that if I shot them in the head enough times, they stopped trying to gnaw out my spleen. And since I'm uncharacteristically fond of my spleen, shooting them in the face seemed like the best option available.

After a few minutes of shooting, Greg and I were the only monsters left standing, and with the little demon girls taken care of, we returned our attention to Bun-head and whatever hell she was trying to raise.

"Oh crap. This is not good," I muttered when I saw what was going on at center court.

"I think we're gonna need a bigger gun," Greg said.

"What the hell is that?" I asked.

"I think Hell is exactly what that is, bro."

That was a huge beast spinning slowly in the air where Sabrina had been floating barely a minute before. It was at least twelve feet tall, with long curving black horns protruding from a bony forehead that looked like a cross between a wolf and a huge bull's head. The monster had arms the size of pine trees, with foot-long claws at the ends of hands the size of Christmas hams. Its legs were human in shape, but bigger around than my waist. It had bare feet with three claws in front and one backward-facing claw, all razor sharp and shiny in the red light. Its skin was red like the little demons, and it had a double row of teeth that glinted as it smiled down at Bun-head. The demon stopped revolving and floated slowly to the floor directly in front of Bun-Head, then smiled down at her with a hundred pointed teeth.

The voice that came out of the demon made my skin crawl. "You have done well, my daughter. Now shed that weak mortal shell and assume your rightful shape."

As we watched, Bun-Head morphed into a female version of the beast. I could tell it was female because it wasn't terribly modest about hiding the eight teats that hung grotesquely off its chest.

"Dude," I whispered to Greg. "Where's Sabrina?"

"Dude," he answered, "I think the big thing is what Sabrina turned into."

"I was really afraid you were going to say something like that." I looked around for the cavalry I knew wasn't coming, drew my backup piece with my left hand, and stepped in front of the beasties. "Hey, assface!" I yelled.

Both of them turned toward me, and I yelled, "Where's the girl, dental nightmare?"

The big one looked down at me. "More minions? Good? I was looking for a snack. I appreciate the tasty virgins you gathered for me. In thanks for your loyal service, I shall kill you quickly."

The female formerly known as Bun-head whispered something to Baal, and he turned to me and grinned. "Never mind. Belial says that you were no help at all. That means I get to play with you a while before I kill you."

Baal stepped out of the remnants of the circle, and I felt the floor shake with his weight. The glowing magical barrier winked out of existence, and there was nothing standing between me and a monster straight out of my childhood nightmares except about twenty feet of faintly brimstone-scented gymnasium air. Whoever first wrote that high school was hell had no idea just how right they were.

"Greg, you got any bright ideas?" I asked without taking my eyes off the demons in front of me.

"You take the big one, and I'll fight the one with all the boobs?" He sounded about as scared as I felt. Neither of us wanted to show it.

"You only want to fight the chick so you can cop a feel and claim you got to second base."

"Yeah, but that would give me a score in a new decade, so I'd be ahead of you." He fired off a clip at Belial's head and then launched himself at the demon. I was amazed to see that he actually knocked her off her feet. I began to think we might have a shot at surviving this after all.

Then I took stock of Baal. As an opponent he was a couple of feet taller and a couple hundred pounds heavier, with muscles in places I was pretty sure I didn't have places. I hoped Greg had enough sense to run like hell when Baal killed me.

"All right, tall dark and drooling, let's do this." I emptied my backup into his kneecaps, and wasn't surprised when he didn't even flinch. Had to try.

I drew my big knife and jumped at the monster, and a second later found myself looking up at a disco ball hanging from the gym ceiling. "Ooooh. Pretty."

Next I saw a massive clawed foot rushing at my head. I rolled to the side before Baal could stomp my head flatter than a fast-food hamburger. His claws dug deep into the hardwood, and all I could think was *I am not picking up the tab for refinishing that.* I kept rolling and he kept stomping until I finally ran out of floor. I expected to feel my brains squirt out my ears at any moment.

This was where we'd find out if pancaking a vampire head is just as good as a decapitation. His foot came rushing down. I'll admit it—I closed my eyes. I couldn't handle the thought of watching my death come in the form of a size forty-eight bunion.

But no squashing happened, just a huge crash a few feet away and a bellow that literally shook the rafters. A volleyball that had to have been wedged up there for at least five years came down and landed next to me, flat and dusty. I opened my eyes, and when I didn't see a demon getting ready to step on me, I sat up and almost wished I hadn't.

Chapter 34

Greg had beaten Belial down pretty hard, but she was fighting back and they were slugging it out at one end of the gym. But the bigger, better weird show was center court, with a glowing sword in his hands. Baal was down on one knee a quarter of the court away, glaring at Phil with glowing red eyes.

"What are you doing, Zepheril? You're one of us!" shouted the demon, and I could feel the heat from his breath all the way across the gym. I could smell his breath, too. Baal seriously needed to reevaluate his dental-hygiene regimen.

"No matter what I've done, I never have been, and never will be one of you, *demon*."

The way he said *demon* was like it was the vilest curse he could throw at something. And maybe to him it was. I'd never seen Phil like that—his wings were unfurled to their full width, at least twelve feet tip to tip, and he wore a kind of armor that almost glowed. It looked old, like a flickering light bulb trying to come on that didn't quite have the juice. His sword, which had hung at his side looking normal in my apartment, had grown to about six feet in length, with a huge hilt and a blade that was blinding white to look at.

Baal glared at him, and after a long minute said, "So be it, angel. Prepare to meet your little God again." And he spread wings of his own, gigantic bat wings that I would have sworn weren't there a few minutes ago, and soared towards Phil with his claws out and teeth bared.

Phil flew back at him, and for a few moments all I could see was the flash of the blade and claws, they moved so fast. Then my attention shifted over to the corner of the room where Greg and Belial were still fighting. She was holding Greg up with one hand and beating his face in with the other. I took a running jump and grabbed Belial's arm and spun her around. She dropped Greg and backhanded me. I stumbled backward, but caught myself and spun into her with a right cross that came from my heels.

Maybe the little nibble I had of Lilith did make me stronger, because Belial flew clear across the gym before crashing into the bleachers against the far wall. I shifted my attention to Greg, who was getting to his feet gingerly. He looked like you'd expect a vampire to look after being used as a sparring partner by a demoness—like a bag of crap.

I crossed the gym to within a safe distance of Belial. "Where's Sabrina?"

"You mean the police tramp?" She hissed at me from what looked like a broken jaw.

Good. I hoped it hurt. A lot. "Yeah, her."

"She's gone, vampire. Gone like the idiot woman that drew me to this plane. She was my final sacrifice to bring my father to this world. You've lost, now. Give up. Die like the sheep you are."

"*Baa-Baa*, bitch," I said, and I emptied the clip on my Glock into her face hoping that enough silver bullets in a small space would be enough to send her back to Hell. Finally, after all seventeen rounds lodged in her frontal lobe, she dropped like a rock. "Looks like those silver bullets work after all." I put a fresh clip in the pistol and turned back to where Baal and Phil had been duking it out in the Main Event.

The angel and the demon were breathing heavily, both looking the worse for wear. Phil had blood oozing from a gash on his side, and there was a hole in his shoulder where it looked like Baal had pierced him with a claw. Baal only had one wing left, and it was hanging in tatters. They were circling warily, each probing the other's defenses. Now and then one would take a cautious swipe with claw or sword.

Phil noticed me out of the corner of his eye and nodded to me slightly. I saw him trying to maneuver around so that Baal would be between him and me, so I could get a clear shot, but Baal just stood in the middle of the gym and laughed.

"It will be a cold day below when you can lead me into that trap, Zepheril." The monster chuckled.

"It was worth a try, demon," the angel replied, a wry smile on his lips.

"Why are you helping these mortals, Zepheril? You've always sided with the winners before now. You know that only the strongest survive, so why are you throwing in with these weak sacks of meat?"

"I picked the wrong side once, Baal. If I've been given the opportunity to correct that mistake, I'll not let it go by."

I flashed back to Sunday School and realized they were talking about the war in Heaven, the big one where Lucifer and all his angel buddies were tossed out after trying to lead a revolution.

Then they were at it again. Faster than my eye could follow, Phil went after Baal with the sword. Baal swatted the slash away with one huge forearm, and lashed out at Phil with his razor-sharp claws. Phil ducked under one slashing blow and stabbed at the monster with his sword. Baal actually caught the blade with one hand, but white fire flowed over his clawed fist and the demon yanked his burned hand back.

Phil followed with a slashing overhead blow, but Baal was too fast, dancing backward with a grace belied by his giant size and massive muscles. Baal lunged forward with both arms, stabbing at Phil with his claws, but the angel spread his wings and flew over his attack and slashed at the monster's back. The blade drew a thin line of white fire down the demon's back, and he let out a howl that blew the glass out of backboards all around the gym.

I saw a split-second opening while Phil was clear and the monster was distracted. I took my shot. Squaring my feet, I emptied my last clip of silver ammo into the back of the demon's head, and had the satisfaction of seeing the beast fall face-first onto the gym floor. Phil landed beside the fallen demon and raised his sword high.

"Nooooo!" I screamed and launched myself at the angel, catching him in a tackle worthy of the Pittsburgh Steelers. We tumbled head over heels across the gym as I tried to keep him from killing Baal.

"What are you doing, vampire?" I looked down when we had stopped to find a very pissed-off angel inches away from my face. He stood up, taking me with him, and grabbed me by the shirtfront. "I had him beaten. I've waited centuries to make this right, and *now* you decide to interfere? What the hell are you thinking?"

"Sabrina," I croaked. He had more than a little throat in his grip. "We've got to save Sabrina. You kill Baal's body, what happens to his host?"

"Idiot! His host isn't even on this plane of existence anymore. She's in Hell, you moron! He traded places with her, that's why you could kill all those little girls without murdering a child. Or didn't you think of that?"

"How do you know?" I know Phil had been around since the beginning of time and all, but some things I wasn't quite ready to take on faith. Phil didn't speak, just waved his arm around the gym. I followed his hand and saw a bunch of dazed little girls where demons had been lying, and an unconscious substitute home-ec teacher sprawled on the bleachers where Belial's body had been.

"Oh," I quietly said. "As you were then, back to the killing big demon things."

Unfortunately, Baal was no longer where we'd left him. Why is nothing ever easy?

Chapter 35

Of course the demon wasn't lying where we had left him, all nicely posed for a killing stroke from an angelic sword. Demons aren't exactly renowned for obedience. That's why they're demons and not angels, I suppose. Baal had gotten to his feet and pulled himself back together on the other side of the gym, with his back to a wall. He looked a little the worse for wear, but only a little. I hate fighting things that heal faster than me, so I made a mental note. He definitely had the edge on me in the healing arena.

I took a quick inventory. I had exactly one knife, a .380 pistol with eight rounds of regular ammo, a Glock 17 without a bullet to be had, and a bad attitude. Phil had a really big, magical sword, and Greg had two fists and a concussion. The more I thought about it, the worse our odds looked. I did what I always do in those situations—I stopped thinking before the odds convinced me to stop trying.

I jumped as high into the rafters as I could and yelled out to Greg, "Go low!" He dove at Baal's feet while I dropped from the rafters on his head, hoping to accomplish something besides getting cut in half by Phil's oversized toothpick. Baal was too fast for either of us, though, swatting us both out of the air like mosquitoes. Really big mosquitoes in Greg's case, but you get the idea.

I managed to adjust my course enough to land on a broken basketball backboard, and turned back to the fight to see Phil wading in with his sword. He and Baal were weaving a deadly ballet in the air over the gym floor, Baal's wing and Phil's shoulder healed enough to make the fight too evenly matched again. Thrust, dodge, thrust, slash, duck, repeat. It was almost beautiful to watch, except for our pressing need to help the angel and get Sabrina out of Hell. I made another mental note to ask Mike's Wiccan friend Anna about different planes of existence if I lived long enough to see her again.

I looked frantically around the gym for something heavy enough to hit Baal with, but other than a pile of shattered party decorations and an overturned apple-bobbing tub, there was nothing of any size lying around. Then my eyes lit on the still form of Bun-head, curled in a fetal position beside one set of bleachers. I yelled over to Greg "Make sure big ugly stays off me, I've got an idea!"

"How do you suggest I do that?" he yelled back.

"Keep Phil alive!" I dashed across the gym. Pieces of ceiling fell around us as Baal and Phil's battle raged on. We were going to have to finish this pretty quickly, or there wasn't going to be anything left of the gym.

I got to Bun-head, reached out and shook her shoulder. "Hey, lady. Janet!" I shook her harder, and finally she looked up at me and screamed. I forgot that I had my fangs on display, and that tends to worry humans, even ones that sometimes summon demons. I slapped her across the face, and she stopped screaming long enough to slap me back.

"What in the world is wrong with you, young man?" she asked tartly.

"Wrong with me? Lady, we don't have that much time. Anyway, do you know how to banish this big red bastard?" I pointed over to Baal, and she turned a really gross shade of pale green. I moved back a little, in case she was going to puke, but she got herself under control. Even as I moved back, I realized the irony of not wanting to get a little puke on me when I was covered in demon brains and blood both demonic and vampiric. But we all have our little hang-ups, and one of mine is being puked on.

"How would I know anything about banishing monsters?" She looked more confused than anyone who had caused this much trouble had any right to look.

"You're kidding, right? Lady, you frickin' *summoned* him! I would think that knowing how to put the genie back in the bottle would be one of the first things they teach you in Demon Summoning 101!"

"Demon summoning? What are you talking about young man? And what is wrong with your teeth?"

"We've got way more important things to deal with right now than my teeth. Like the fact that the big red guy over there is Baal, an Archduke of Hell, and that you summoned him, and now I need you to put him back where he came from because there is a very attractive lady cop that is currently hanging out in Hell, where Baal is supposed to be, because when he came here, she had to take his place down *there*. Are you getting this? *Hell*. An innocent woman in Hell."

I was pretty proud of the fact that I hadn't hit her yet, but she was running out of time before I started punching things, and she was the nearest target.

"I did no such thing, young man. I am a Christian! I merely called up the angels to assist me with a certain problem, and nothing more. I would never consort with demons! I won't even speak to agnostics!"

"What 'certain problem' were you calling angels to help you with?"

She didn't answer.

"Cancer? Are you sick? Do you have a sick kid?"

Still nothing.

"Were you praying for peace? Trying to bring soldiers home and bring those families back together?"

Not a peep.

"*Then what the hell was it?*"

"The lottery." She said it so quietly that I almost didn't hear her.

"What?"

"I asked the angels to help me win the lottery. It's up to $165 million, and I could use the money to do so much good."

"I bet you could. If you live long enough to collect and if there are any people left to help."

I couldn't believe it. A string of kidnappings, a zombie infestation, a pile of demon possessions, a parking lot full of trashed cars and a gymnasium that looked like Armageddon was just the opening act, and it was all for money. Root of all evil in-flippin'-deed. "When you called these 'angels' did you use a spell or pray?"

"I found a spell to communicate with celestial bodies. I used that." I heard a huge crash from behind me and chanced a look over my shoulder. Baal had thrown Phil through the DJ setup at the end of the gym and the angel was getting up, scattering CDs, turntables and speakers every which way.

"Well, great job, lady! Look how well that's worked out for everybody!"

"I didn't mean to!" She was almost crying as what she'd done started to sink in. I took a deep breath, looked back at where Greg and Phil were holding their own (barely), and settled myself down.

"I know. And you can make it right. Do you know how to banish this beastie?"

"I have no idea. I don't remember anything since Tuesday night. I was walking home, and all of a sudden I was asleep. I had the most terrible dreams, too."

Crap. Tuesday was when we fought the girl at Tommy's house. When Mike banished Belial, she must have followed the magic back to her summoner and taken her over. Bun-head remembered nothing since Belial took over and started trying to bring Daddy Dearest to Earth in earnest. That meant she wasn't aware when Baal was summoned.

"Stay here, then. And if that thing kills us, start running."

"Where will I go?"

"I don't think I'm going to care very much if I'm dead. If I croak, you're on your own. And maybe even if I don't croak."

I stood up, centered myself and got ready to jump back into the fight. Then, out of the corner of my eye, I caught a glimpse of something shiny. I'll admit that I'm easily distracted by shiny objects, but this time my "attention to detail" paid off.

At one side of the gym there was a little stage set into the wall, and at the front corners of the stage, one on each corner, were two flags. One was the standard American flag with an eagle atop the flagpole, but it was the other flag that caught my eye. I recognized it from playing softball for a Baptist church one summer in high school. It was the Christian flag, a red cross on a field of blue in the top left corner of a white flag. More importantly, the flagpole was eight feet tall and topped with a heavy gold cross. It looked like just the thing to smite an archdemon with. I looked around the gym quickly and saw no better option. It was time to see if this theory about holy objects really held.

I ran across the gym and grabbed the flagpole, pleasantly surprised when it didn't burst into flames at my touch. Okay, maybe vampires aren't all that unholy. What about demons? I yelled over to Greg, "Get high!"

He vaulted about fifteen feet into the air, and I chucked the flagpole at him like a javelin. He harnessed all of his vampire abilities, caught it on the fly, turned a somersault in midair, and dove straight down for Baal, cross first.

Phil saw what we were doing and launched into an all-out attack, thrusting and slashing with renewed fury. I had a brief second to think about how screwed we were if this didn't work, and then Greg was diving into the demon with his Christian flagpole/spear. As the flying vampire got close, the cross atop the flagpole began to glow, eventually bursting into white fire as it touched the demon. Greg buried the cross deep into the meaty part between Baal's head and shoulder, and the demon collapsed to his knees, screaming. Greg landed behind the beast and rolled clear, as Phil moved in for the kill.

He paused for a second, sword raised, and Baal looked him in the eyes. "Why, Zepheril? You could have been the greatest of us all."

Phil looked at him with something like pity and said, "Milton was wrong, Baal. It is infinitely better to serve in Heaven than to rule in Hell. I hope this proves that I've learned that lesson." Then Phil drew back his sword and sliced off the demon's head in the middle of the gym.

Chapter 36

After such a brutal fight, the aftermath was almost anticlimactic. There was no big explosion, no huge lightshow as the demon vanished into sparks, no great gaping maw opening in the earth to suck Baal back into Hell. All in all, it would have been much more impressive if it were designed for the Xbox. But real life, as weird as it is, still isn't a video game.

So the demon disappeared, to be replaced by a screaming Sabrina standing in the gym firing her pistol randomly around her. We all ducked, and she ran out of ammo without shooting anyone on this plane, so all was good.

I waited a minute before I stood up cautiously and said, "Sabrina? Are you okay?"

She looked at me, still holding her pistol, and said in a shaking voice, "Jimmy?"

"Yeah, it's me. Are you okay?" I repeated, more slowly this time.

"I . . . I think so. I mean, I'm back. I'm alive, or at least I think I'm alive."

"Trust me. You're alive. I can smell you."

She wrinkled her nose. "I'm sure I smell like Hell."

"Literally, but it beats being dead and smelling like zombie."

She laughed, which worried me a little. I always worry when a woman laughs at my jokes. When they're laughing *at me*, it's situation normal. But when they're actually laughing at my jokes, I look around for the camera crew.

"So, it was Hell? I didn't imagine that?" Sabrina limped over to one of the tables that had been scattered around for the carnival and sat down.

I followed her and stood beside her. I kept looking around, worried that we weren't quite done fighting for the evening.

After all, it wasn't quite midnight, so I figured there was still a chance for everything to go to crap at the witching hour.

"Yes," I said simply. "I'm pretty sure you were in Hell."

"I believe it."

"What was it like?" She hesitated, and I added, "If you can talk about it, I mean."

"Yeah, I think I can. I was surrounded by those psycho little girls from the forest again, and no matter how many of them I killed, more of them kept coming. They swarmed me again and again, and when I finally thought they had killed me, I opened my eyes and I was standing there in the forest again, and they were all coming again. It was like *Zombieland* meets *Groundhog Day*."

She shivered, and I moved beside her and put an arm around her shoulders. "You know, Bill Murray was in both of those movies. It's clear you have a thing for my type."

She elbowed me in the gut, but she laughed a little. That was twice she'd laughed at my jokes. We were gonna need a hospital for her pretty damn quick. She was obviously concussed if she thought I was funny.

Then her smile died. "What happened here?"

I gave her an accounting to the point where Phil cut off Baal's head. When I got to that part, I stopped and yelled across the gym. "Hey, Phil!"

"Yes, James?"

I guess I'd acquitted myself well enough in the fight, I'd been promoted past *little vampire*. "Why did you help us?"

"I told you. Baal was a danger to us all."

"Uh huh. You're a fallen angel, right? Cast out of Heaven for picking the losing side in Lucifer's rebellion? Stuck here on Earth forever because you can't go to Hell and you'll never be allowed back into Heaven?"

"Never is a very long time, Jimmy-lad. And we're not given to see all the way to the end of time." Mike limped into the gym, one arm draped over Lilith's shoulder as she helped him to our table. "Even the worst of sinners is offered redemption, again and again."

Greg and Phil made their way over to us, as did Bun-head, who introduced herself rather shamefacedly as Janet.

"That's a nice fairy tale, Mike. Not necessarily true." I pulled a chair over next to Sabrina, and she didn't pull away. That's always a good sign.

"You made enough peace with your maker to come onto holy ground to fight a demon. Who's to say there's not hope for even a fallen angel?" I shook my head a little, but I generally defer to Mike on spiritual matters. After all, he's the one with the hotline to the Guy Upstairs, not me.

"Hey!" Greg's head snapped up. Even with his vamp healing, he looked rough. His fight with Belial took a toll. Greg had a black eye, which looked about three days old. Split lips were healing, but still seeping a touch. If he felt anything like he looked, then he felt like he'd been killed all over again. His eyes were clear, though, and something had obviously struck him.

"How did you get in here? And what about you?" He asked Phil, and then Lilith. "I thought you couldn't set foot on holy ground without bursting into flames or something."

"That was him. I'm not a fallen anything, little vampire. I can go anywhere I like. I just didn't want to get involved in your little mess." Lilith looked at all of us smugly, obviously pleased she'd been the only one who hadn't been possessed, nearly killed or beaten to a pulp by a demon.

Phil glanced over at Lilith, then sighed and let it pass. "I couldn't set foot on holy ground, but once Baal set the demons free and stepped out of the circle, the gym was no longer sanctified. The very touch of a demon corrupts any place that it alights, and only the holiest of places can withstand that touch. This place was not nearly holy enough to stay sacred with an Archduke of Hell walking around. Rescue became possible."

"And I guess Janet here could come in because she was still a human being, even if there was a demon driving the bus, so to speak. But why was Baal so disappointed in you? The boy was torqued." I wasn't sure he was going to answer me, but he and Mike exchanged a look, and then Phil took a deep breath and started to talk.

Chapter 37

"I suppose after sharing the field of battle, you've earned an explanation," Phil said. "Long ago, in the dawn of mankind, there was a war in Heaven. Lucifer and an army of angels decided that humans were being given too much rein over this world, and that God needed to be deposed. I was one of those angels."

"How'd that work out for you?" I asked. Greg elbowed me in the ribs and I shut up.

"Not well. We were defeated, obviously. The rebels who repented and promised to serve loyally were given their places back in the Host, while those of us who stood by our principles were cast out, forced to live among you worms as a constant reminder of exactly who the favorite children really were. And Lucifer was sent to rule in Hell. He took nine of his closest compatriots with him, and they became the Archdukes. Baal was one of them."

"Wait a minute," I interrupted. "Baal was once an angel?"

"Haven't you been listening?" Phil looked at me like a disappointed teacher, which is a look I was all too familiar with. I love getting put in my place by angels. It's like adding insult to insult somehow.

"Baal joined Lucifer in Hell, and I became one of the Fallen here on Earth. I watched your civilizations, as if the word were even applicable, rise and fall. I watched your societies mature and decay, and over time I came to realize that I had been not only a fool, but a coward as well." The angel stopped and took a breath. I got the feeling he'd been waiting a long time to tell this story, but hadn't had the right audience.

"I couldn't return to Heaven, and I couldn't go to Hell. I was trapped here until I could do something to warrant an audience with the Father again. I had to do something to make him notice me, to remember me, so I could tell Him . . ." Phil's voice trailed off and he blinked rapidly.

"Tell Him what, my son?" Mike asked, and I saw him as his parishioners must see him, as a wise man, a holy man. My oldest living friend almost glowed with an internal peace that made even me want to confess to him.

But we didn't have all night.

"That I'm sorry and I want to come home," Phil said quietly, shoulders tense and head bowed.

"Just ask Him," Mike said so gently I was afraid for a second that Phil was going to cry.

Phil fell to his knees right there in the gym, and Mike joined him. The rest of us followed suit, except for Lilith. Mike looked over at her, and raised an eyebrow.

"I don't kneel. Ever. To anyone. It's my thing." She sat down at the table, leaned back in her chair and propped her spike-heeled boots on the table.

"He knows," Mike said. "He knows." Then he took Phil's hand. "Now, Phil. Ask Him."

Phil looked up and one tear ran slowly down his cheek. He took a deep, shuddering breath and choked out, "Father, may I come home?"

I'd never seen Phil look contrite before. Of course, I'd never seen him cry, or fight a demon before either, so it was another night of firsts for me. Yippee, another learning experience.

"I think," Mike followed the angel's gaze with his own "all you ever had to do was ask." Then Mike put Phil's hands together and raised them straight over his head.

Nothing happened for a moment and then Phil began to glow with an incredibly bright, white light. I could only stand a few seconds of the glare, and even squeezing my eyes shut I knew I'd be seeing spots for a while. When the glow faded, I opened my eyes, and Mike was standing there, with no angel beside him.

Lilith looked around for a minute, and then muttered,

"Sonofa*bitch*! He didn't leave me any instructions other than to take care of the club."

"What does that mean?" I asked. She treated me to a look that could kill someone who was actually living.

Lilith took a deep breath and said, "I owed Phil a debt. Since he didn't absolve me of it, I'll have to keep his business operations running until he does, or until the period of my service comes to an end. So I'm stuck here for a while."

"How long?" Greg asked. He kept trying to sneak peeks up her skirt as she leaned back in her chair, but he was about as subtle as a hand grenade.

"Five hundred years, minus time already served," Lilith answered.

"How much time have you served?" I asked.

She shot me another look. "Two weeks."

I looked around at Greg, Mike and Sabrina, and we all burst out laughing. After a few seconds, Lilith got up and left without so much as a good-bye. She did not strike me as a woman who was accustomed to being laughed at, which could go badly for us. Chances were we'd have to deal with her for the next few centuries.

Chapter 38

After our little chuckle, I sat up straight and looked at Janet. "So how do you plan to put all this right, lady?"

"What is there to put right?"

"What is there to—*what is there to put right?* Your little spell goes wonky and a passel of little girls end up kidnapped, a dozen zombies tear up most of Charlotte, a cop—"

"Detective," Sabrina put in.

"—detective gets sent to Hell and we trash an entire private school gymnasium. And all because you wanted to win the *Powerball!* That's what I mean, you nutjob!"

"You're asking for the impossible. I can't possibly do much to change things. But for starters I promise never to do magic again, even the kind that summons angels."

"Demons," I corrected.

"Well, I meant for it to summon angels. That nice man at the Career Day explained it all to me. The spell would summon the angels, who would perform three wishes for me—"

I held up a hand. "Wait a minute. What nice man at Career Day?" I had a sneaking suspicion I knew which "nice man" she was referring to.

"Mr. Arthur. He runs a chain of tire stores. We got to chatting about how school funding kept getting cut, and vocational education was getting hit worst of all, and he gave me a prayer book that he said would summon angels. But it didn't so I must have done it wrong! But I really wanted to help, doesn't that count for anything?"

Everyone around the table yelled in unison "NO!" I made a mental note to have a long conversation with the Tire King about the difference between angels and demons someday very soon.

Janet had the good grace to look ashamed, even if she didn't have a good answer. After a long moment, Greg broke the uncomfortable silence.

"Hey, look. The sun's going to be coming up soon, and this building is no longer what I would consider light-tight, so at least a couple of us would like to get home. The rest of you are welcome to crash at our place if you like, but we need to get going."

"I can't," Janet said. "I have to get home to Mr. Kibble. He must be frantic with worry about me."

"Don't worry. You weren't really invited. And who the hell is Mr. Kibble?" I asked.

"My Pomeranian. He's very high-strung and gets terribly nervous if I don't make it home in time for dinner."

"Whatever. Look, lady, I'm keeping an eye on you, and if I so much as see you buying the wrong color candles near the summer solstice, they'll have to identify you by your dental records. You got me?" I gave her my best intimidating stare, which was helped a little by the blood spattered all over my clothes.

She nodded and scurried out the door before I remembered that she might not have an intact car in the parking lot.

Then I couldn't manage to care. Oh well, now that she wasn't possessed by a demon, I figured the rest of her problems would pale in comparison.

"What about you two?" I asked, looking at Mike and Sabrina.

Mike shook his head, "I've got to get to the church for morning Mass, but I'll swing by later for lunch. I'll drive you, though. My car is still in one piece, and I moved it right up to the gym entrance."

"I'll come hang for a little while, as long as there's no biting while I nap," Sabrina said, standing and holding out a hand to me. I took it and she helped me up. I didn't really need it, but the feeling of her warm hand in mind wasn't something I was likely to pass up.

"No promises on the biting," I said as we started toward the waiting car.

Greg limped past us, leaning on Mike and yelled "Shotgun!" over his shoulder at us. I didn't mind.

"There's just one thing I don't understand," I said in a low voice as Sabrina and I walked down the steps into the parking lot. The eastern sky was barely beginning to lighten from black to deep blue, so it was definitely time to get rolling.

"Just the one thing?" she asked.

I punched her lightly on the arm, and she staggered a few steps sideways. Sometimes I forget that I'm not punching Greg.

"When you were taken, and Mike got thrown out of the gym, he mumbled something about you being an innocent."

"Yeah?" She had that look that women get when I'm about to ask something that'll get me slapped.

"And if I remember right, there were certain criteria for being a sacrifice to raise this demon, and one of them was a very specific brand of innocence."

"Yeah?" she repeated, and unlike Mike, Sabrina had obviously mastered the art of raising only one eyebrow. She was either daring me to go there, or warning me not to go there. *What to do? What to do?*

"So by being part of the sacrifice, does that mean..." I trailed off and Sabrina interrupted me.

"Let's put it this way, Jimmy-boy. If you finish the question, you'll never know the answer." She kissed me lightly on the lips, and we got in the car and rode off into the sunrise like good vampire heroes.

About the Author

John G. Hartness is a recovering theatre geek who likes loud music, fried pickles and cold beer. He's also an award-winning poet, lighting designer and theatre producer whose work has been translated into over twenty-five languages and read worldwide. John lives in North Carolina with his lovely wife Suzy and writes full-time.

CPSIA information can be obtained at www.ICGtesting.com
Printed in the USA
LVOW042055040113

314477LV00005B/17/P